THE WOMAN WHO WROTE *KING LEAR,* AND OTHER STORIES

The Woman Who Wrote "King Lear," and Other Stories
By Louis Phillips
ISBN 978-1-929355-39-6
Library of Congress Control Number: 2007937936

Design by Susan Ramundo
Cover by Laura Tolkow

Pleasure Boat Studio books are available through the following:
SPD (Small Press Distribution) Tel. 800-869-7553, Fax 510-524-0852
Partners/West Tel. 425-227-8486, Fax 425-204-2448
Baker & Taylor Tel. 800-775-1100, Fax 800-775-7480
Ingram Tel. 615-793-5000, Fax 615-287-5429
Amazon.com and **bn.com**

and through
PLEASURE BOAT STUDIO: A LITERARY PRESS
www.pleasureboatstudio.com
201 West 89th St., Ste. 6F
New York, NY 10024

Contact **Jack Estes**
Fax: 888-810-5308
Email: *pleasboat@nyc.rr.com*

For Pat

Who made the writing possible &
Who deserves so much more than these

love

TABLE OF CONTENTS

Errata

In last month's issue, we were privileged to publish a new short story by Louis Phillips. The story, as you may remember, was titled "Errata," and it has elicited thousands of letters expressing admiration for its grace, style, and felicity of expression.

Unfortunately, as the author and numerous irate readers have pointed out, the story contained a small number of printer's errors. The printers' and editors' strike of last month has finally been settled, and so we hope to resume our unusually high standards of careful proof-reading, but we feel that we should bring to your attention the errors that occurred in last month's story:

TITLE PAGE: The author was Louis Phillips and not Nathaniel Hawthorne.

PAGE ONE: The main character was Mr. Malone, not Ms. Malone.

PAGE TWO: Pages Two and Three got reversed in the editing process. Page Three should be Page Two. Page Two should be Page Three. All other pages, however, are correctly numbered.

PAGE TWO (old Page Three): The sentence that reads, "Mr. Malone was ravished by Mr. Phillipott in a hanging garden where a dead moose was rotting," should read, "Ms. Malone was not ravished by Mr. Phillipott in a hanging garden where a dead mouse was rooting."

PAGE FOUR: The paragraph that reads, "So saying the fair and hospitable dame took our hero by the hand; and the touch was light, and the force was gentleness, and though Robin read in her eyes what he did not hear in her words, yet the slender-waisted woman in the scarlet petticoat proved stronger than the athletic country youth. She had drawn his half-willing footsteps nearly to the threshold, when the opening of a door in the neighborhood startled the Major's housekeeper, and leaving the Major's kinsman, she vanished speedily into her own domicile."—actually comes from Hawthorne's "My Kinsman, Major Molineux." How this unfortunate interpolation came about is difficult to explain, though it has been pointed out that the same firm that typesets our stories was also in the process of setting type for an anthology of short fiction by American authors.

In your edition of "The Woman Who Wrote *King Lear* & Other Lurid Tales for Readers Drawn to Sex and Violence on an Operatic Scale," please delete Mr. Hawthorne's paragraph and substitute the following: "Major Phillipott, father of Amos and beloved husband of Robin, a fair and hospitable dame, was indeed haunted by a terrible sin. The Fall of Mankind was no abstract theological concept to the Major's tortured soul; the Fall occupied the very center of his Ground of Being. One could trace to the Fall, that most important moment in the history of the world, the Major's major obsession: he hated mistakes. He despised slovenliness. He attacked minor errors with the same loud enthusiasm used to dispatch the Arabs at Khartoum (General George Gordon, the Egyptian governor general of the Sudan, had been Phillipott's childhood hero). His mornings were frequently spent dictating heated letters to the London *Times* or to the Manchester *Guardian*.

Once when he found a nightshirt left over the arm of a chair, the Major flew into a rage. Since the nightshirt belonged to the hapless Amos, then only ten years of age and far away from his tragic episode with Ms. Malone and the dead mouse, the Major ordered his son's entire wardrobe burned. The servants, blushing under a flurry of grotesque orders, gathered together every shirt, pair of trousers, all socks, shoes, underwear, suspenders, ties, vests, and corsets, and they piled the clothing in the front lawn.

In front of the weeping Amos, Major Phillipott doused the freshly starched materials with a container of kerosene and he lit the match himself.

Unfortunately, the conflagration got entirely out of hand. A surge of wind took the group by surprise. Trees, grass, hedges, two servants, and eventually the manor house itself were badly singed. Major Phillipott, too proud to admit that he himself had committed an error of judgment, refused to place a call to the fire department; but as the fire was spreading to the upstairs bedrooms, the Major's wife, bravely fighting off hysteria, attempted to call for help. Alas, Amos, in great anger because of the unjust humiliation heaped upon his now naked shoulders, had severed the telephone cords with a pair of hedge-cutters stolen from the gardener's shed. The shed, in fact, was the only out-building left standing. In a frantic last-ditch effort that bordered upon desperation, Mrs. Phillipott, nee Sedgewick, retired to her bedroom and dictated a letter to her secretary, a certain Ms. Malone (who shall play a much larger role later in our tale), a slender-waisted (wasted?) young woman, who created something of a scandal in the major's household by her frequent sportings in a scarlet petticoat (the very same petticoat found in the field near the dead mouse). The letter was addressed to the Suffolk County Department of Pyrotechnics and Fire-tending:

To Whom It May Concern:

My husband, the Honourable Major Horace M. Phillipott, has accidentally set a fire that now threatens our estate and manor house and all the valuables they contain, including the Major's collection of rare postal errors (inverts, over-printings, and incorrect colors). I therefore humbly beg your department to send out your fire-wagons as soon as this epistle falls into your hands.

Warmly yours,
Robin H. Phillipott (Mrs.)

PAGE SIX: The two pages of stock market listings are not part of the story proper. They were inserted by mistake.

PAGE SIX-A: The sentence that reads, "Amos Phillipott joined a nudist colony, and he refused to wear clothes for the rest of his life, while his mother moved to London to work as an assistant to a producer of stage plays," should have read *"cautere sur une jambe de bois."*

PAGE EIGHT: There is no Page Eight. As far as we can tell.

PAGE NINE-A: The name of the main character was misspelled. The correct spelling is Amos Phillipott. Please correct throughout.

PAGE TEN: The bird identified as a Ruby-Crowned Kinglet was incorrectly identified. The bird that Amos saw, while frolicking in the field with the secretary, was, in all probability, a fulvous tree duck.

PAGE ELEVEN: The sentence should read, "Ruddy ducks have been known to cock their tails." We wish to apologize to all readers who were offended by the obscenity that resulted from an irate editor's transcription.

PAGE XII: The recipe calling for twelve pounds of raisins should be replaced by the following sentences that were inadvertently dropped from the main body of the text: "It was not until nearly two decades after the death of Major Phillipott (he died from inhaling kerosene in the back seat of his Rolls while the automobile was on fire) that the now-Lady Phillipott finally met her son in one of the high-priced nudist camps that dot the shore of Southern France. *Cautere sur une jambe de bois,* she thought but did not speak because she was thinking in a language she could not pronounce. She did not at all feel embarrassed walking naked, hand in hand with her son. But she finally realized how wrong-headed her husband had been in burning her son's clothes. There are some experiences a family can live without.

PAGE 16 and 3/4: The final page of the story somehow blended into the beginning of Linda Bucknell's article, "Ten Things To Do with Your Son or Daughter on a Hot Summer Day." The final sentence of the story should read, "When it came night, the white waves paced to and fro in the moonlight, and the wind brought the sound of the great sea's voice to the men on the shore, and they felt that they could then be interpreters." Delete: "Give into the ecstasy of endless love." Delete: "Build a stove from scratch."

ADDENDUM

Ordinarily we would be pleased to reprint the story in its correct form, but we feel that in this unusual case that there were so very few errors involved, and all of the minor variety, and that the story itself was somehow enhanced by the additions made—well, we have printed the errata sheet. We allow each reader to judge for himself/herself.

Suddenly I Do Not Equate the Light with Anything But Madness: The Best Short Story of 2010

If you look through THE BEST SHORT STORIES OF 2010, you will find my story there. It won first prize that year, beating out some pretty good company. Joyce Carol Oates was there with a story about beating up Philip Roth, and Philip Roth was there with a story about beating up Joyce Carol Oates, and John Updike was there with a piece about Rabbit beating up himself and going to Heaven and meeting both Joyce Carol Oates and Philip Roth. I'm telling you that the writing game is a pretty rough business and very political. What the poor say is true: It's not what you know, but who. Whom?

How I found out that my story had been printed, however, is a story unto itself. But we all have stories unto themselves and, the longer I live, the more I think that all of our stories are pretty much alike. It is as if you woke up one morning and carried with you all the voices of the world. Such voices stick to you, and no matter how hard you try you cannot shake the voices off. "*Alles ist innig.*"

"Didn't the editors tell you that they were going to print your story?" my father asks. John is having quite a difficult time reading the pieces because the sun is in his eyes, bouncing off the page, and my father is too proud or too lazy to go inside to get sunglasses. Or maybe he does have sunglasses and the sun is in my eyes so I cannot make out the title of my own story. I know I had sent the story to somebody, but somebody didn't like it. The story kept coming back.

Then one day it didn't come back anymore. I had gone to the Police Station to swear out a Missing Documents Report, but the police, up to their ears in Neo-Platonism, held out no hope for its return. "So many stories disappear every year," the sergeant said. He was a kind man, in his early sixties and on the edge of retirement. He had seen stories of all shapes and sizes walk off the face of the earth. Three years ago they had uncovered an unpublished fragment by Holderlin in a warehouse in New Jersey. The fragment had been left in storage by Warner Brothers.

Of course, by the age of 36, Holderlin had gone insane. No wonder. "*Alles ist innig.* Just because it happened to Joyce or to McCullers or any of those other guys, it doesn't mean it's going to happen to you," the sergeant said.

He didn't mean to be unkind. He was merely telling the truth. Just because it happens to someone else it doesn't mean it's going to happen to you. Actually he reminded me of my father. I left Precinct 23 with about twenty posters. (The missing document artist had reconstructed my story to the best of his abilities, but in truth my powers of description were woefully inadequate. There were so many touching passages missing. No one could hope to identify the story from the outline on the poster). The only part that made any sense at all was the making of my child.

In addition, the posters from the police station were printed upon white paper. It is difficult to take seriously a story printed upon white paper, even if the story does concern a father and a son digging up the corpse of the boy's mother so that the body can be moved to another cemetery. Such a story does not make much of an impact nowadays. We are interested in something else. And we all know what the philosopher G. E. Moore says about the assertion that Blue exists: "If we are told that the assertion 'Blue exists' is meaningless unless we mean by it that 'the sensation of blue exists,' we are told what is certainly false and self-contradictory. . . . We can and must conceive the existence of blue as something quite distinct from the existence of the sensation. We can and must conceive that blue might exist and yet the sensation of blue not exist. For my own part I not only conceive this, but I conceive it to be true." For my part all I do is look up at the sky and see that it is sometimes blue; though, of course, I realize that even sky blue is an illusion. An illusion like so many stories, so much memory. My mind is mostly blue movies.

I look across my mother's grave and see that my father is wearing a blue work shirt and blue jeans. He's in his late seventies and he can still put in a good day's work without complaining. He used to be a carpenter, but now he builds odds and ends for friends and neighbors. Don't whine, just do it, he would tell me when I was a child. I believed him then. I believe him now.

"Didn't the editor even tell you they were printing your story?" John asks me again. I have wandered off into my own thoughts. I have been doing that a lot lately, much to the distress of my friends. I am burning out, but I can't stop. Too many papers to grade. Too many part time jobs. The honor of being recognized for a story that is not even mine has come too late, much too late to do me any good at all. It is about as much use as a toothache, though to tell the truth I have had a toothache all week, and I am beginning to enjoy it. Its pain is weaning me into real life, luring me away from complacency. I go over the Catechism of Stone in my head. The Catechism of Stone is a series of ideas about the relationship that exists between a stone and the hand that throws it, a catechism my father and I have frequently recited to each other, though often when my father gets drunk the catechism eludes him, and "The Shooting of Dan McGrew" ends up in its place. How often do we start off with one story and end up with another? You only have to read *The Best Short Stories from 2010* from cover to cover to know the answer.

"Therefore," says Simonides, "I shall never spend my allotted span of life vainly in infeasible hope, seeking that which cannot come to pass—a fully blameless man. None of us who win our bread from the wide earth. . . ." People are talking to me all the time, and I never know what to say in reply. Orchids. I suppose one could say "orchids" in reply. One could open one's mouth and pull out flowers. "ονδε μοι εμμελεως το Πιττακειον / νεμεται, καιοι σοφου παρα φωτος ει– / ρημενον χαλεπον φατ εσθλον εμμεναι. / θεος αν μονος τουτ εχοι γερας, ανδρα δ ονκ / εστι μη ου κακον εμμεναι, / δν αμηχανος συμφορα καθεληι / πραξας γαρ ευ πας ανηρ αγαθος, / κακος δ ει κακπς," quotes my father, tossing down his shovel and reaching for a bucket. Ironic that he almost kicks the bucket in a literal sense. It's his idea that my mother's body should be dug up and moved to Syracuse for reinterment. She should be near her parents, my father insists. When you die you should go back to your family. He's old, and so that's the way he thinks about things, not the way G. E. Moore thinks about things, say, the color blue, or Holderlin, or Simonides. We think things; we say things; we forget them. I am forty-four and angry all the time. How does the commercial go about G. E. Moore? *G. E. brings good things to life?*

Three feet into the tender earth, my mother, my father, and I have encountered an underground spring, and the water flows into the grave so rapidly that we must bail like crazy.

"*Sonavabitchingflyingfuckingwater.*" My father swears a blue streak. Up one side of the grave to the other, with both of us standing in the muck and mire, mud slopping into my one pair of shoes. The spring gurgles like a demented child crazy with happiness that it has done something to thwart the best-laid plans of mice and men. "Bail, bail, bail," my father mutters to himself, and then glares at me as if the water pouring over the remains of his dead wife is somehow my fault because he knows that I am superstitious and do not want the body moved.

"*Sonavabitchingflyingfuckingwater.*" The hidden spring flows in at such a slow rate that my father and I, working in tandem, each of us bailing as if we were in a leaky boat—where we have been more than once in our lives—can undo it, work beyond it and bring my mother or what remains of her to the surface.

"You can slow down now," John says. "We got it licked."

Overdoing it! That's what I want to do. I want to come on with everything and crazy and break the skull of the world wide open. I'm a madman all right and I don't care who knows it. Alas, Yorick.

I pick up my shield and run my hand over its convex front. It is the kind of shield called a Goolmary. Long. Heavy. The back of the shield is nearly flat. In spite of the July heat, I know I must dress in full armor. To tell the truth I need a new shield. A man should not go into new battles with the same old weapons. A trip across town is in order. There the washer woman waits. She too up to her arms in water. "No," I said. "I think the editors wanted it to be a surprise."

"Is it?"

"Of course," I say. "But to tell the truth I am embarrassed."

"I would be too. It's not well thought out. Something essential is missing. I wanted to cry and there is nothing to cry over, and what's all that stuff about going crosstown on the bus with the passengers babbling about loneliness. Loneliness is not everything."

"It's not even mine."

"What do you mean?"

"Something's wrong. They have printed someone else's story under my name."

"Are you sure?"

I think about that. It is a worthwhile question. One I dig my rotten tooth into. "That's what bothers me. Maybe I wrote something and I have forgotten all about it. The world is filled to overflowing with stories. Some of them might belong to me."

I know I shall have to walk across town and confront the publishers. Perhaps the bald-headed editor has confused my story with one told by someone with a similar name. A tale told by an Id. Waiting for mother to dry, I call my brother to ask what he thinks.

My brother delivers baked goods to restaurants and delis. "I took Saturday off," he tells me over the phone, "and now I have to pay for it. The dispatcher is giving me a bomb of a schedule." He volunteers to make a new shield for me, but I would have to arrive late in the afternoon. His bomb of a schedule does not permit him to return home before sundown. My father says he'll come along later to help.

"Hand me my axe," I say.

"Huh?"

"The Hortuk."

John hands me my Hortuk. The axe feels good in my hands. One of my brothers—there are six of us—had brought it back for me from Malay. I adjust my helmet and pick up my spear. One takes one's gifts where one can.

"You really have to go across town?" my father asks.

"I have no choice. I've been humiliated. Publicly humiliated."

"The public doesn't care. It's not a movie."

"But I do."

I place a few stones in the pocket of my shirt.

I take the book with the story attributed to me from John and start across town. The bronze of my armor glitters in the sun. There is a good chance I shall lose ten or twenty pounds on this one trip alone. Not that I mind. I can afford to lose the weight. I have been running to fat. Too many palindromes: *A I rot sack Castoria.* What a mind! If it were only mine. We are born with too few minds.

I walk a few blocks and then decide to conserve my energies by taking the bus, although I knew that many passengers would be miffed by the presence of my shield, spear, and axe. Weapons meant for slaughter always take up more room than anybody thinks. Standing on the crowded bus I reviewed what my father and I had learned from the Reverend P. H. Francis. In his book on *Mechanical Biology,* the Reverend Francis had written:

1. The stone by itself is an incomplete weapon: the complete weapon is formed by the hand and stone together.
2. The contrivance formed by the hand and stone has many features of the fist.
3. The contrivance consists of two main parts: a human part formed by the hand, and a mechanical part formed by the stone.
4. The form of the hand and stone are complementary. The contrivance is wielded in much the same way as the fist.
5. The hand is released by the stone from the need for directly delivering the blow.
6. The type of weapon formed by the hand and stone depends on the way the contrivance is used and on parts which come into contact with the opponent.
7. The fastenings which hold the hand and stone together are formed partly by the hand and partly by the stone.
8. The human and mechanical parts of the fastenings holding the hand and stone together are complementary.
9. The contrivance is held to the arm by fastenings formed by the fingers and their connections to the arm.
10. All actions and movements of the body are affected by the partial replacement of the fist by a stone.
11. Advantages gained by partly replacing the fist are accompanied by disadvantages.

In W. H. Auden's poem "The Shield of Achilles," he creates an image of a boy throwing a stone at a bird. Did such a boy think of all the ramifications of his thoughtless and mean-spirited act? Was he aware that the human and the mechanical parts of the world are complementary?

On the bus two passengers, women in their early eighties or their hundred-and-twenties, were discussing an article about testing loneliness on the Differential Loneliness Scale.

"How did you do, Milly?" the woman in the moon mask asked.

"I flunked the course," said Milly. "I always do. It was the question about keeping all the lights at night burning that got me. Who can afford to keep lights burning all night long?"

"Who can afford lights?"

"You can say that again,"

"But to measure loneliness," Milly said after a while. "I never thought that they could do it."

I get off the bus three blocks from my brother's garage. My armor glitters in the sun. A world of bronze amid a world of steel. A world of greed. Oh, mother, why didn't you make me immortal?

I am surprised to find my brother hard at work. My father is at the door to greet me. No matter where I go, he is always waiting for me. I don't know how he got across town ahead of me. "I told the boss what he could do with his bomb of a schedule," my brother says, bent to his welding. The garage houses many curious items, among them a complete hand-carved carousel. The floor of the carousel is covered with grease. My father slips and slides, and I hold out my hands to pull him up. He is getting old and it takes everything in my power to keep him going. Asking him to help my brother Edwin to build me a shield might keep his mind off decay, how his own body is failing him. I wonder what he thinks about being a father, but I don't ask him. Instead I ask him about the water in the grave. "When I reached your mother's body," he says, turning the bellows toward the fire, "she had turned to stone. All except her head. The head has disappeared."

"Her head?" I ask. I use my arms to wipe the sweat from my face. "We'll have to go back and look for it."

"Later."

My brother doesn't say anything. Like me he is upset about moving my mother's body to Syracuse. But now her body is like stone and sinking further and further away from us.

"When I first buried her," my father continues as he and Edwin lift my new shield from the forge, "she couldn't have weighed more than 150 pounds, but in her present state I wager she weighs at least twice that."

Life's funny. One minute you're nothing but a son. Then the next moment a being emerges from the darkness into the light and you are both father and son, a member of a generation caught in the middle. One generation was being pushed off the edge of the horizon. Another embarking on the cruise.

"If you're going to do battle with the publishers," my brother says, "you're going to need stones."

"I've got them," I say, "in the pocket of my shirt."

"They don't fight fair."

"I know."

"They don't have to."

"I know."

"How can they publish somebody else's story under your name?" he asks, as he brings his hammer down upon a huge rim of bronze. My mother's face shines. It is as if she is speaking. The artist has made a miracle.

"Must happen all the time," I say.

"Remember, if you throw stones, that the human and mechanical parts of the fastenings holding the stone and hand together are complementary."

I nodded. "Number 8," I said.

"What should I put on this shield?" he asks. Edwin is in his late thirties, and his eyes are brown like mine. His back is straight. He works without stopping, the sweat pouring from his tanned face, his hair glowing red hot in the foreground of the forge.

"Start with the creation of the universe," I told him, "and work your way down."

"You always were the ambitious one in the family."

"I know."

"On the other hand. . . ." My brother's voice trails off.

"I know," I tell him. And my father, staring at my mother's face upon the shield, bursts with a cry of grief, such a lament that every goddess gathers about him: the Nereides of the wine-dark sea; Glauce, Thaleia, Nesaea, Speio, Thoe, and ox-eyed Cymodoce; Doris, Panope, and Galatea of the spiriting song; Nemertes beating her breasts; Doto, Pherusa, Limnoreia, Ianeira, Ianassa, Maera. Each pulls John from the grease-stained floor; each fills the grotto with grief and prayer. My mother's body has turned to stone. She weighs more in death than she ever weighed in life.

On the shield my brother has depicted a wedding dance. And there are my parents, seated in chairs, being carried around and around in a circle. And then there is my father's heart besieged by two armies. The first army has sat outside his feelings for ten years or more. There on the imperishable bronze, amid the dancing and the feasting, is a lone singer. Bent to his guitar, he sings a song not of his own making. His heart rises into his mouth. Soon all the dancers stop in their mad whirlings and they listen. The singer sings:

Well-met, well-met, my own true love,
Well-met, well-met, says he,
I've just returned from the saltwater sea,
And it's all for love of thee!

I might have married a king's daughter fair.
In vain she'd have married me,
But I refused a crown of gold,
And it's all for love of thee.

If you could have married a king's daughter fair,
I think you are much to blame,
For I have married a house-carpenter,
And I think he's a nice young man.

The song is published under his name but is not his, and the singer turns red with fury. He lifts his guitar and smashes it to the floor. The music breaks into many pieces. The wedding guests are embarrassed.

Edwin turns back to the forge. Nothing he can say or will say can assuage my father's grief. And there on the five-layered shield, tears are falling. What can fathers tell their sons? What can sons tell their fathers? We live under the fear of loss. One losing the other.

The great Orion. I place my arm through the strap at the back of the shield. Edwin knows what he has made; I do not know what I have made. That is the great difference between us. Two sons from the loins of one man, and yet we have so little in common.

"Kill them," Edwin says. "Kill them all. I hate all those bastards."

"I will," I say. I find a spear on the greasy floor and, using a discarded rag, wipe the shaft clean. I dip the point into poison.

"Wait!" John says. "Before you go. I have to tell you something about your mother. A story you haven't heard." I reach down and pull him up.

"When the telephone company installed the first pay phones in Manhattan, your mother walked into Howard's drugstore to try to call home. The operator told her that it would cost her a $1.05 to talk to her home in Syracuse. And so you know what your mother did?" John can hardly contain himself. He starts to laugh long before he gets to the good part. I glance over my right shoulder towards Edwin. He and I have both heard the story before. Most of my father's stories about my mother are pretty much alike, except for the most recent, the one about her body turning to stone and her head disappearing. What was the best way to define what any family was? By the stories that were repeated from one generation to another.

John stops laughing long enough to continue. He requisitions number 76432243876554 from Chestnuts Unlimited, his ears turning red. "And so the operator keeps telling your mother to deposit the money into the slot and your mother keeps insisting that she has put the money into the phone and after a few minutes of wrangling back and forth, Mother gets it into her head that the phone company is trying to cheat her and so she goes out to get a policeman to press charges against the phone company. And when she dragged the policeman back, she showed him where she had placed a nickel in the nickel slot and a dollar bill in the dollar slot, and as soon as the policeman sees that he nearly doubled over with laughter."

I look at my watch. The illustrious lame god was dogging it past midnight. The Pleiades. The Wain. John Wain. What a mind! If it were only mine. Donovan's Brain on recall. My father, having finished his tale, picks up his shovel and goes forth in search of my mother's missing head. My brother takes my outdated and outmoded Goolmary and tosses it to the scrap heap. I turn my attentions to the battle at hand.

Edwin places his hand upon my shoulder. "You know that story John tells abut Mother stuffing a dollar bill into a pay phone and pushing it down into the coin slot with a hat pin? Well I found it in an old newspaper the other day. It never happened to Mother at all."

"Why does he insist on telling it then?"

"You ask him."

"No, you ask him. You're on better terms with him than I am." Edwin wipes the sweat from his face with a greasy rag. Poor Edwin, I think, always besieging his father's heart, and all to no avail. Melancholy sets in like a greased pig, its eyes rolling back in its head. They both make things with their hands and maybe that's what keeps them so far apart. The pride of craftsmanship. Overhead the dirty ducks called Zodiac. If the gods did not create humans there would be no stories to tell, and of course, no television at night to while away the whiling hours.

2. *The Night Interlude*

My tooth has started to ache. At the Protagoras and Meno Publishing House, owned by Dodgem and Ketchem and Makem

Cry, where the ghost of Hemingway slugs it out with Fitzgerald for the right to be slaughtered by graduate students and associate professors with hairs in their nostrils, there is only one small light burning. Someone is trying to outmaneuver the big boss, the *Times'* literary critics, the marketing analysts, the Zeitgeist take-over bureaus; another penny into the slot of mass illiteracy. No wonder Richard Corey went home one summer night and put a bullet in his head.

Storm clouds gather on the rim of my shield; bolts of lightning beg to be thrown, but where are the lightning throwers of yesteryear? Must file a missing lightning report. Precinct 23. The point of my homemade spear glistens in the moonlight. Or perhaps I must conceive of the existence of moonlight as something quite distinct from the existence of *experiencing* the moonlight. Walking alone through the city of moonlight I remember a story my father had told me many years earlier of a man who had seven children and what happened to him when his wife walked out on him, leaving him to look after the brood. He delivered ice for a private company in the city of Baltimore and one morning he went insane. He tossed all his ice into the streets, huge blocks of ice that temporarily, at least until they melted, stopped traffic, stopped traffic cold, you might say. And then he started throwing his ice-picks and hatchets at the horses who pulled the wagon. He threatened to kill the horses if anyone came near the wagon or tried to stop him. "I'm going to kill the whole goddamn family!" he cried. The wife had run off with a boy eleven years younger than herself. And the man on the ice-wagon, with seven mouths to feed, went insane. Who could blame him? And who could blame me for what I was going to do to Dolon or whomever I caught, I who have stood outside the walls longer than any Greek now enter the walled city and walk slowly down the marble corridor, past the scrub lady kneeling by her bucket, half the known world dissolving into slop, the chieftains united in some guise of sleep, past the windows with the gold lettering—Peisander Iphidamas. I stop, glance at the silence, adjust my belt under my cuirass, find the solitary light, pull out a few stones. Stones in one's hand are as good as words tonight. Stones will bring the enemy down. The scrub woman takes one look at my blood-hungering spear and swishes the ammonia with a sudden violence. She nods her head toward me, granting me permission to go ahead. She hates the men who exploit her as much as I do, or is she Athena in some pathetic disguise? How does one tell a goddess but by the back of her knees?

Through the windows of the 209-story building, I see the moon being hurled through space like a small block of ice, or a yellow stone worn down by eons of evolution. Baseball: *Alles ist innings.* Number one: The short story by itself is an incomplete weapon. The rich have only one goal: to keep the poor poor, to keep weapons and the means of production out of the hands of anyone who is not a member of their club. And how does one become a member of their club? One becomes them. *And no sooner had the words left his lips, an incomplete way of telling, a madness if you will, when Peisander took a spear deep into his breast.* I kick open the door and place my body into the frame, throwing a stone over the editor's desk.

A humpbacked man with a bald head and a green eye shade looks up, startled.

My stone shatters the naked light bulb. Broken glass splashes down, filaments of astronauts over manuscript pages of Holderlin, or some story about Norman Mailer beating up Hemingway, and James Jones smearing Styron's body with chicken blood, the two of them rolling over the bones of Capote. It's a rough business all right because no one can ever give you what you want.

The editor hastily strikes a match. Who are you? What do you want?

By way of reply I fling the *Best Short Stories of 2010* across the bulb-littered desk. "Do you see this story?" I ask. Bellow. Bellows like Saul. *Suddenly I Do Not Equate the Light with Anything but Madness.* Who wrote this thing?

14

The editor lights another match, opens a drawer and pulls out a stub of candle. I fire another stone through the glass door that reads *Ilus, Managing Editor.*

"Please don't break any more windows," Dolon cries out. His adverb-bitten knees shake. "Every piece of broken glass comes out of somebody's salary. Another poet bites the dust."

"Who wrote the story?" I ask, pushing the man backward with my shield. I'm surprised to be confronted by a white-haired man. In many respects he reminds me of my father. Usually publishers hire young ladies fresh out of college because the publishers don't have to pay them anything. No wonder most publishing houses can't spot talent if it came to them in a chariot of fire.

"Your name is on it." His face is white with panic. Pre-french-fried.

"You know it's not mine!" I shove the man to the ground and place the spear point to his throat. His Adam's apple goes up and down as if trapped in a windy elevator. The editor bursts into tears. "Don't kill me," he pleads. "Take the money from the cash register. We hold onto royalty money until hell freezes over. Take the interest from the accounts of our authors. No one will ever miss it. Then go. Consider yourself blessed that we even allowed your words into our sacred text."

"Pull yourself together, man!" I tell the man, baring my fangs. "You know they weren't my words. I don't write such convoluted stuff. Divine simplicity is what our age demands. MTV. Saturday Morning Cartoons. Sit-coms masquerading as full-length plays."

"My parents will be glad to pay any ransom you demand." My spear is beginning to draw blood. Splotches of red appear on the collar of the editor's Brooks' Brothers shirt. A few bright drops stain his logo. We can and must conceive the existence of blood as something quite distinct from the existence of the sensation of bleeding.

"Who wrote it?" I demand, pushing the razor sharp blade to the blue-penciled flesh. If we must stop and think about the meaning of every word, every action, nothing will get done. Nothing.

"I did! I did!" he shouts. Or the words shout. I retreat slightly all the better to hear his sordid confession. This is what I have come to hear, but in my step backward, my shield-bearing arm accidentally nudges the yellow stub of a candle on Dolon's desk, and the candle topples over. Up in flames *swoosh* goes the latest work of Salinger. His autobiography heats the sterile office. All his letters crawling out of copyright.

"Fire!"

"Don't change the subject," I say. "Why did you put my name on a story that was not mine?"

"Because I thought it would be a way for some writing of mine to see the light of day." At the opened door standes the washer lady with a bucket of kerosene. She tosses the content onto Salinger's *Autobiography*. I guess the washer woman doesn't believe in that David Copperfield kind of crap either.

"Run for it!" the editor shouts, using his striped-shirt arms the way a sailor might to semaphore a drunken and inept moon. And there they were: the carpenters fluttering with Peter Cottontail. The sprinkler system is set off and the water rains down from the ceiling. Bail, bail, bail. I guess Salinger was particularly angry about the nude photos of himself published in *Playboy* magazine.

"No. Recite for me the Catechism of Publishing. Quickly." The shaft of my spear grows so hot that I can barely hold it. It glows in the darkness. The farmland on my shield drinks in the water from the sprinklers and bursts into life. Life! And oh how its tooth aches.

"The contrivance known as fiction is formed by hand and electrical energy. They both have the many features of the fist. Two: The mind of the writer and the reader are complementary. Three: All actions and movements within the work are affected by the partial replacement of the story by the critical faculties of the reader.

Burn ye tarriers. Burn!

The type of story formed by reader and writer depends upon the way the contrivance is used. I drive the point of my spear through the editor's throat. *Well met, well met, my own true love.* It's difficult to surprise editors because they have read so much. His eyes bulge. Black vomit sprays across his shirt. I place my foot upon his stomach and pull out the spear. The point brings with it bits and pieces of his windpipe. I kick him in the groin and then turn him over so that he lies face downward. Perhaps if he lies in the water long enough he shall turn to stone. Dangling modifiers are burning through the rip in his shirt. Now I think he's a nice old man. The washer woman has long ago vanished. The staples crackle. Vanished.

When I reach home, my father has left a message upon my machine. He has removed the headless body of his wife from the water-soaked grave and tomorrow he will place her on a train and accompany the body to Syracuse. But, of course, that is another story. *The reader is released from the story by the need for directly delivering the blow.*

Vanished.

Writing

⌒

"Writing. Or the Night of the Falling Hairs." I have to type these pages with no looking back, because the lynch mob—complete with torches, wheelchairs, hangman's noose, waterboards, tar, meteors, and postmodernism despair—has gathered upon my front lawn. They are the threatening to burn my house down. I have no doubt that they will make good their treat.

Why me?

It must be that the fair citizens of Arkansas have discovered that I am the one who has been writing. Buck Harness yells, "Lynch him! Lynch him!"

Fiction writing of course is against the law. It always has been. It drains the economy. It steals time from the ordinary affairs of living. Letter writing too has been rendered obsolete. The punishment for writing letters is a mere fine. Writing about writing, of course, is tolerated. And writing about writing about writing. That is because of the Uniform Scholarship Act of the last century.

But the citizens of Arkansas have discovered that I am the one who has been sending them letters exhorting them to read. They resent that. They resent any sort of intrusion into their private lives. Whatever private lives they have. Lives without humor. Lives of no deposit, no return. Lives without any sense of lightness. Quickness.

Jill Fanwell. Ted Slotri. James Merrick. Orin Bridges. Homer Tryphon, in his wheelchair, brandishing one of the large torches. The entire Uriah Family. All ten of them.

They hate it when I write.

And Hank, Bill, and Boggs.

* • *

Not too long ago, Willa Cather was browsing in our public library, when she picked up a magazine, a journal more likely. The journal, which contained all manner of writings and which shall remain nameless here, contained an article—an essay more likely. The essay was called "Why Willa Cather Revised 'Paul's Case': The Work in Art and Those Sunday Afternoons."

Ms. Cather, Miss Cather more likely, knit her brows and read the article straight through. From start to finish. I, sitting in my usual green chair in the bibliographical section, watched her. I always kept my eyes on authors when they came into the library because they were like relics, like dinosaurs, and of course all wore the gray pants and vest proscribed by the State. Miss Cather was no longer allowed to write, but she was entitled to one day per week in the library. The Council of Elders thought it only humane that authors be allowed to wander in from off the street and wipe the dust off their miserably useless creations.

For a small town, the Carnegie Library was well stocked and up to date, though by up to date I mean to say that the latest periodical was dated in the mid 1990's. Miss Cather frequently found items to amuse her. This morning, however, plodding through the fossils of her literary past, she was not amused. The librarian and I clearly heard her sighs. "I thought I revised my stories because I wanted to make them better. Count on strangers to discover more subtle motives."

She closed the journal and carefully returned it to the proper place upon the shelf. She was always very good about that—

returning materials, books more likely, to their proper places. Thus, she was always a great favorite with the Head Librarian.

On the way, Miss Cather, donning her simple brown jacket, nodded to me. I nodded back. We never spoke. I could never get up enough courage to speak to her. But she was always very polite. That's one thing I always like about her. I quickly took down the journal she had replaced and read over what she herself had read. I, of course, not being so personally involved, not the one being dissected, did not sigh. There are many advantages to not being in the public eye.

Tonight I sigh. But for different reasons.

* • *

I write upon the blackboard over my bed twenty-five times: *Postmodernism despair postmodernism despair postmodernism despair postermodernism postdespair post this pair poster modern Is M despair? postmodern despair premodern hope.*

The crowd on the lawn has swelled. The children chant: "Burn him. Burn him. Burn him. Burn him alive." Children who have barely learned to walk have learned the alphabet of despair. The alphabet book of hate ("A" is for AGAINST everybody who does not believe what I believe) has such pretty pictures in it.

* • *

I love picking up books and running my fingers over the letters. How many times have the letters of the alphabet been compared to bugs or to insects?

In an essay for *Esquire* (1988 or so), Mark Jacobsen remembers "books with letters that looked like crushed insects going backward."

In *Tarzan of the Apes*, when Tarzan returns to the wrecked ship that had brought him to Africa, Tarzan discovers some books, among them a child's primer. Although the pictures fascinate him, he is most taken by the letters of the alphabet which he thinks of as bugs: "The strange little bugs which covered the pages where there were no pictures excited his wonder and deepest thought."

I stared at pages and pages of bugs. What will happen to them when they heat up? Will they fry? Sizzle? Let us barbecue an alphabet of sense.

I place another piece of paper into the typewriter. Since the mob downstairs is in no mood for considered conversation, I have decided to write them a letter, a page covered with red and black bugs (my writing machine is so ancient, a 1941 Smith Corona, that I am able to outfit it with a ribbon that writes both black and red. Probably not unlike the machine that Mark Twain used to type out one of his manuscripts. He was the first American writer to turn in a typewritten manuscript to his publisher. We still call them *manu*scripts even though they are no longer handwritten—hence, "manu"—in pen or pencil. Pencil: Manual Graphite Information Processor):

Dear Mob:

Even though you burn me and my house to the ground, you will not have defeated me. By acting like mad animals, you will have only defeated yourselves. You are playing Creon to my Antigone. I beg you to reconsider your actions. For the good of yourselves. For the good of our children. Yours till the cows come home.

Sherburn

I read the letter over several times. There is something magical, mystical more likely, in starting with a blank sheet of paper and ending with a bug farm. What can be better than writing?

I take my note, fashion it into a paper airplane and fly it out of my attic window. I watch it float to the ground where seventy-year-old drunk, white-haired Boggs retrieves it. It then occurs to me that nobody on the lawn may be able to read. So many words coming to nothing. I would be better off cutting out my heart and flinging it through the window. Let them devour it whole.

What are words but ways of disguising one's heart?

* • *

In my collection of letters from publishers to authors, I pull out a folder. My collection has always been a source of great amusement to myself, and no doubt Buck Harkness and his cohorts would like to see my papers go up in smoke as much as anything else.

A letter to H. G. Wells from his publisher:

My Dear Mr. Wells:

Thank you for sending us your latest manuscript, *The Visible Man*. As much as my colleagues and I have enjoyed reading it, we find that your basic premise—a scientist discovering a cream that allows him to remain visible to his fellow human beings—is not one to excite our imaginations. Is that not what language is for? To allow us to remain visible to our fellow human beings?

We would, of course, be happy to consider any revision you come up with. Suppose he discovers some drug or substance that renders him *in*visible. Does that sound like a viable premise? Would such a plot appeal to you?

Please know that our offices always remain open to you and your efforts.

* • *

Please know that our offices always remain open to you and your efforts. It may have been centuries before when an author heard that phrase.

I smell something on fire and so I go to the window and look out. Under the oak tree, I am being hanged in effigy. My straw figure clutches a sheaf of papers, letters more likely. Letters I had written to my fellow citizens.

Dear Buck:

Have you ever considered reading *Huckleberry Finn*? I believe you will find Chapter XXII quite amusing.

Yours,
Sherburn

* • *

I think before I am burned alive in my own house, surrounded by millions of bugs and tons of papers, I should confess the most shameful incident of my life.

It has to do with writing. *Not* writing, really.

When I was in my teens, I had been working as a delivery boy for some television store when I chanced to knock upon a motel room door. The room was inhabited by a family of gypsies. There were three men, five women, and about a half dozen children all squeezed together inside one tiny bedroom, with walls decorated with reproductions of blind puppies and castrated kittens.

After one of the men, the oldest and best dressed of the lot, signed for my delivery, he asked me if I could write?

"Could I write?"

"I mean," he said, "could you write a letter for us?"

"Write a letter for you?"

"Yes," he said. He was embarrassed. He was a handsome man, straight-backed with a white mustache, but he could not look me in the face. There was so much about life I did not understand then.

"You see," he said, trying to be as casual as possible, while the other gypsies remained in the background, looking over his shoulder, "we need to send a very important letter home, back to Hungary, letting our friends and relatives know that we are all right, but we cannot write. Would you write it for us? We will pay you, of course. What would you charge to write a letter for us?"

Knowing what to charge for one's writing is a very difficult problem. I am nearly a half century old, and I still do not know how to solve it. How could a boy in his teens answer?

The other day a man was offered $10,000 for a cereal box. For a cereal box! Empty, but with the picture of a losing football team upon it.

"No, I'll do it for free," I said.

"No. We'll pay you. When can you do it?"

"I'll come back this afternoon," I said.

"Five?"

"Five." Though how that family would ever know the time was beyond me, for no one seemed to be wearing a watch. Nor did there seem to be any clocks in the room. No radio. No television. No books. Did they ever venture outside? How did they pass the time? Three men, five women, a half dozen assorted children gathered into a single motel room—each one waiting for me to come back, to save them from their destiny, their Fate. Though Camus, in his essay on Don Juan, insists that "a fate is not a punishment," that day it was. For I said I would return, but I did not.

I never wrote the letter for them. The punishment has been constant.

Why didn't I return after my errands? Was I afraid? No doubt. I had heard rumors of kidnappings performed by Gypsies. And yet if I had done them a favor, they would have been in my debt. They would have perhaps given me a charm or chanted a secret saying to protect me from harm, to keep my house from burning down.

But I never went back to them. I never wrote the letter. Perhaps someone else did. I have frequently tried to imagine just what they wanted me to write. Suppose I had become implicated in some crime? Of all the shameful acts I have done in my life, and I have done many bad things, that it is the one act of which I am most ashamed. Is that not strange? What sin had I enacted? A broken oath? A promise not kept? Hell, I've broken a lot of promises, I bet. For what is talent but a promise? And what is unfulfilled talent but a broken promise, a promise between one's self and one's soul. And I thought I wouldn't look back.

Please know that your Past always remains open to you and your efforts.

* • *

The Night of the Falling Hairs. "Sherburn, come on down here and get what's coming to you," the mob on the lawn shouts. The night air is filled to overflowing with the smell of burning.

"We got your paper airplane note," shouts Ted Slotri, "and we don't know what in tarnation you're talking about."

"It's you that's been sending us all those letters, urging us to break the law!" Boggs shouts. He has worked himself up into quite a rage.

And so too has the night sky. The sky is filled with Leonid meteors. A meteor shower so bold, so all- encompassing that even the mob has to step back and take notice. For a moment their insanity is distilled into watching. Even I cannot take my eyes off the tremendous hairs of light that stream through heaven. The Mayans, who had seen such a sight thousands of years before and who had chiseled their records into stone, thought that the hairs had fallen from heaven with Tzontemocque, the Lord of the Dead.

On November 12, 1931, a clergyman in Russia also witnessed a shower of meteors. He wrote: "I saw a large number of angels shooting from the sky with fire-like arrows."

From records chipped into stone some six hundred years before the arrival of the Spaniards in Mexico, to the ravings of a mad priest (angels, no less), we look upon the same phenomena—births, marriages, deaths, meteor showers—but we do not describe them the same way. What we describe, more or less, is who we are.

I turn away from the angels shooting arrows, and rummage deeper into my files. I cling to papers the way a rat clings to a moldy bit of cheese. Everywhere I turn are papers and more papers. The writing at night breeds more writing. Words give birth to more words. Ah, the Alphabet! Even a Mayan one.

A letter to Robert Louis Stevenson from his publisher:

Dear Mr. Stevenson:

Thank you for bringing you latest manuscript to my attention. I must admit that my colleagues and myself certainly enjoyed the ingenuity behind your lurid account of *The Adventures of Dr. Jekyll and Mr. Jekyll.* Unfortunately, we do not think that there is a great enough difference between the two personalities. The fact that one holds a Doctorate while the other does not probably will not carry much weight with the ordinary reader.

Since Schizophrenia is all the rage these days and is certainly a subject to make money with, we would be most happy to consider any revised manuscript you wish to send us. May we suggest that you make the difference between the two characters more apparent—perhaps give each character a separate name. For example: Dr. Jekyll and Mr. Hyde. During the day, Dr. Jekyll could practice his medicine, but, at night—ah, at night, when the air is filled with meteors— he would believe himself to be a young boy. Perhaps he would be attracted to the river. He could build a raft and then, should you be in need of an ending, he could drown. Or he could be a werewolf. Werewolves are in this season.

I hope you do not find the above suggestion too presumptuous.

Sincerely,
JE

* • *

Since I have told you of what I am most ashamed, I shall now share with you the time I was most afraid.

When I was twelve years old, I was the spelling champ of my elementary school, and because I was champ, I was invited to take part in the county finals. The winner of the county would go to the state, and the winner of the state would go to Washington, D.C., and try to become the best speller in the nation.

I loved spelling. I can still see clearly the first time one of my teachers wrote with chalk upon a blackboard. She was a nun and she wrote with a clear bold hand the word *Family*. Today, of course, all spelling is done automatically on the prose-cleansing machines, and so children frequently miss the excitement of placing one letter after another, one small bug followed by another small bug, followed by even more bugs.

Anyway, one night my father received word from his brothers and sisters in Massachusetts that his mother had died. To keep his sorrow under control, he picked up a 9th-grade speller and he and I sat outside under the stars. He would call out a word and I would spell it, though how he could make out the words in such near darkness was more than I could understand.

After we had been outside for about a half hour or so, he looked up into the Florida sky (we didn't move to Arkansas until nearly a decade later) and he saw a strange circular pattern of lights. It was not normal astronomy. The lights appeared to be going around and around.

A flying saucer, my father thought.

We went inside to call the police.

When my sisters, who are four and six years younger than I, heard that there was a flying saucer outside, they began to cry. They were nearly hysterical. I too started to panic. My mother turned pale. She was trying to keep us calm, but we would not be stilled. The tiny house seemed to vibrate with unspeakable possibilities.

Who would land?

Who would take us far away from ourselves? What would they do to us? What did they look like? Would they use the same language?

My father started out the door to look at the saucer, but I begged him not to go.

I never felt such intense fear in my entire life. Such a taking on.

And my father, what was he thinking of? He had to fly north for his mother's funeral? Would he return to us?

And my sisters and I crying, crying. And I was too old to cry.

Scared to death.

It was awful to see.

* • *

"They swarmed up the street towards Sherburn's house, a-whooping and yelling and raging like Injuns, and everything had to clear the way or get run over and tromped to mush, and it was awful to see. Children was heeling it ahead of the mob, screaming and trying to get out of the way; and every window along the road was full of woman's heads, and there was nigger boys in every tree, and bucks and wenches looking over every fence, and as soon as the mob would nearly get to them they would break and skaddle out of reach. Lots of women and girls was crying and taking on, scared most to death."

* • *

I reach down into the Robert Louis Stevenson folder and pull out two crumbled white pages covered with black ball-point pen ink. It is a letter from my mother, the last letter written before my own father's death. All of this was before the recent legislation.

Dear Son:

All is fine here. Daddy did have a little upset, but is ship-shape now. Just had a check-up. He's okay.

Don and Jill called the other night. Denise had a baby boy, 8 lbs.

Spent an afternoon with Bob and Kay. They are okay.

The weather has not been great down here, very little sunshine. Expect Eunice, Maureen, and Philip on the 26th of the month.

Philip might stay with a friend, Maureen, a week and Eunice and Philip two weeks.

Had a letter from Leslie, sounds like she is very busy. Am sure you have heard from her.

All our love,
Mom and Dad

* • *

If I could figure out why I save all these letters, I would understand who I am. We write to people. We write about people.

Perhaps I am merely a creation in someone else's writing.

Anything is possible, they say. The crowd below is growing. Their chants are unspeakably loud. The idea of them lynching anybody is amusing, I think.

When I go to get my double-barrel shot gun, which I keep behind my filing cabinets, I think about some graffiti scribbled upon a wall at my old school.

My mother went to this school and now she drives a truck. And someone underneath had written: *And what did you go to this school for?* Then somebody else wrote: *To become a truck driver.* Then another hand: *How much does she make?* Different writing: *Grow up.* Another hand then scribbled the ultimate question: *Is she happy driving a truck?*

After thirty years, I still remember that graffiti, when more important writings have fallen by the wayside. Of course, there shall come a time, when the sun burns out, when all writings, even the officially sanctioned ones, will fall by the wayside.

With my shotgun in hand, I climb out onto the roof to face the crowd. I don't say a word. I just stand there, looking down. Quite a few of the crowd members drop their eyes and look at their boots.

I just had to laugh. Most of them didn't want to come.

* • *

"You didn't want to come. The average man don't like trouble and danger.

"You don't like trouble and danger. But if only half a man—like Buck Harness there—shouts 'Lynch him, lynch him!' You're afraid to back down—afraid you'll be found out to be what you are—cowards— and so you raise a yell, and hang yourselves onto the half-a-man's coat-tail, and you come raging up here, swearing what big things you're going to do. The pitifulest thing out is a mob; that's what an army is—a mob; they don't fight with courage that's born in them, but with courage that's borrowed from their mass, and from their officers. But a mob without any man at the head of it is beneath pitifulness. Now the thing for you to do is to droop your tails and go home and crawl in a hole. If any real lynching's going to be done, it will be done in the dark, Southern fashion; and when they come they'll bring their masks, and fetch a man along. Now leave—and take your half-a-man with you."

* • *

And so the crowd washes away. As does the sky. Even the night sky doesn't look the same. I crawl back inside and start another letter. I have told you of what I am most ashamed. And I have told you when I was most afraid.

What more can I tell you?

Writing . . .

The Gorilla and My Wife

There's no sense in pulling punches. I'm a gorilla. I'm not entirely to blame either, but I need to make it perfectly clear to each and every one of you that animal magnetism is a force that is not to be taken lightly. Though hindsight is the spinal-cord of history, it is obvious to me now that I should never have, under any conditions whatsoever, allowed my wife and myself to enter into the foolish experiment under the direction of Mr. Sherril L. Collyer, direct and unalloyed descendant of Robert H. Collyer, who, at one time, as reported by some benighted knight of the keyboard, had "nerves to withstand ridicule, power to quell opposition, an iron constitution, an indomitable spirit, and magnetic power in a remarkable degree. He boldly entered the field, predicated himself on truth, defied attack, challenged the opposition, and has won for himself imperishable fame." The fact that Robert H. Collyer is hardly a household name today leaves the notion of his imperishable fame in some doubt, though I confess I still speak of him. Nor can it be denied, especially by me, not entirely in my right mind, that Sherril has inherited considerable powers from his indomitable ancestor. Such are the joys of heredity.

Why I allowed the foolish experiment to take place, and in front of an audience no less, is difficult for me to imagine, though a gorilla's imagination need not be inferior to a man's, at least to some men who shall remain nameless. However, if I remember correctly—

and I have always prided myself upon a supreme mnemonic ability, based in part upon an esoteric Egyptian code—three weeks before the above-mentioned experiment, I had been discussing with Sherril a passage from that rare and highly distinguished pamphlet *The Confessions of a Magnetizer, Being an Exposé of Animal Magnetism,* in which the anonymous author writes:

> Reader, let me tell you that to be placed before a young and lovely female, who has subjected herself to the process for the purpose of effecting a cure of some nervous affection or otherside, to look into her gentle eyes, soft and beaming with confidence and trust, is singularly entrancing. You assume her hands, which are clasped in your own; you look intently upon the pupils of her eyes, which as the power becomes more and more visible in her person, evince the tenderest regard, until they close in dreamy and as it were spiritual affection—then is her mind all your own, and she will evince the most tender solicitude and care for your good. You will then become not only as a law to her, but it is the greatest happiness to her to execute your smallest wish; she is perfectly happy (unless your natural temperament and habit differ widely) in the strange sympathy that now exists between you. Self is entirely swallowed up in the earnest regard that actuates the subject and she will stop at no point beyond which she may afford you pleasure, should you indicate it by thought or word.
>
> Now I ask you is not this a most dangerous agency that can so subject the most upright minds to the will of the unprincipled and oftentimes immoral practitioner?

I ask you the same question.

I have read the passage quoted above some seventy or eighty times since the experiment, but I still have no understanding why the prophetic implications did not sink into the very ground of my being, though I can postulate a number of possibilities. First, I am a highly skeptical 20th-Century man, or at least I was. I have bathed in Existentialism, teethed on Kierkegaard (that guardian of the church), stumbled over Hedonism and Relativity, parsed the grammars of technology, and applauded my ability to knuckle under the disciplines of higher education. In short, I am prone to mysticism.

As I mentioned earlier, I am not entirely to blame, for Sherril Collyer himself has been a friend of my wife and me for years and he has entertained us with hours of gossip culled from the great and the near-great for whom he casts horoscopes. They come through his portals all hours of the day and night, and the stories he tells about them would fill columns of a newspaper. I myself have plotted blackmail with him, but only in jest, of course. Still, for years my wife and I have been privileged to attend a number of Collyer's experiments with mesmerism, hypnotism, animal magnetism, or what you will; and though the experiments did provide me with some amusement, I often *taunted Sherril—taunted* is probably too strong a word; *teased* should be closer to the mark I should think—hinting, in broad tones so that he would get the jest, that he had paid his subjects beforehand or that the persons under his spell were mere confederates to provide us with some small entertainment while our planet plunged blindly on to oblivion.

But ninety-three days ago, almost ninety-four as the clock on the mantle is nearing midnight, the scene described in that brilliant but highly obscure pamphlet of confession did come to pass. Sherril Collyer sat down before my wife, gazed into her green eyes, and in a matter of moments, Claudia gave herself up to the powers of another mind. I did too for that matter, but I must make it perfectly clear that all the time I was under his spell, I knew that I was in control of my senses, and I knew that many of the actions he was commanding me to do were moderately ridiculous. I simply did not have, at the time, the necessary interest to refuse him.

Now the ways of inducing sleep into a willing subject are many and oftentimes elaborate. The famous James Esdaile, for example, had his subjects lie completely still in a darkened room before he would begin his hypnotic passes. Or in Egypt, where a highly obscure sect, not the same one that developed my mnemonic code by the way, has practiced the art of hypnosis for some four thousand years, the method is quite unusual, although quite similar to the ones employed by Sherril Collyer. Two overlapping triangles are drawn or scratched upon a white porcelain plate, and certain cabalistic phrases are scratched within the triangles. The plate is then dipped into a vegetable oil so that the figures and words take on a surprising luster. A subject who gazes intently at the shining plate for a few minutes will soon fall into a deep trance.

To be perfectly accurate, and no one at the Beinecke Library has ever called my accuracy into question, my friend does not use a porcelain plate. What he does use is a shining, semi-transparent amulet with the overlapping triangles and cabalistic phrases inscribed within. The cabalistic phrases are most important, but should I record them here, I may be tempting some unwitting subject down forbidden paths, and this I must not do. My own poor condition is a case in point. If one could only imagine my craving for vegetables and fruit.

For years it had never occurred to me that I should be a good subject for an experiment, for I know myself to possess a strong and independent mind. The first hints that I might be susceptible to hypnotic suggestion occurred three or four days before the notorious experiment, when Sherril brought to my house *The Confessions of a Magnetiser*. He had brought the pamphlet so that I could appraise its condition and worth, with the thought that our library might purchase it for the collection. I say in all modesty that my reputation as a Bibliophile is unsurpassed even in this intensely intellectual community. Indeed, after reading the pamphlet, which was in excellent condition but I am afraid of not much worth, I became quite curious about my friend's little hobby, and so Sherril agreed to try a few simple tests upon my consciousness. While my wife Claudia was upstairs taking a shower, Sherril placed his long, well-manicured finger upon the back of my hand, upon the vein between the second and third knuckle. He gazed intently in my eyes and told me that I would soon feel a great warmth, a tingling sensation. I must confess that my thoughts were not entirely upon the experiment but were in part upon the fact that Claudia was upstairs taking a shower. She had been deliberately avoiding Sherril and it was beginning to disturb me. Sherril and Claudia had always been close friends, but now their friendship appeared to be cooling. For what reason I could not possible imagine. Had Sherril neglected to tell us an important bit of gossip? And so I was concentrating on how to prevent further embarrassment to Sherril about my wife's refusal to put in an appearance or at least to say hello when I did begin to feel a soothing warmth under my friend's finger.

His second 'test," as he labeled it (not nearly so elogant a word I should think) was to have me clasp my hands together. Then, while he stared in my eyes, he said that I would lack the strength to pull my hands apart. I really had the strength to pull my hands apart. I did not feel that I lacked the muscular coordination to pull my hands apart. I merely did not have the will to do so. After all whether or not I could or I couldn't wasn't really important, and so it came to pass that I passed both tests commendably. Thus, it was not a complete surprise to me that Sherril called upon both Claudia and myself to assist his little stage show. I admit my wife was hesitant, especially since she had been avoiding him for weeks, but so many people around her were urging her to take part that she found it difficult to refuse. Surrounded by friends and colleagues and leaders of the business community, my wife and I certainly had no desire to appear as bad sports. Also, I did not wish my wife to enter a somnambulistic state without my being there to accompany her. Whatever malicious rumors are being circulated about me now, I do not wish my chivalry to go unnoticed. Perhaps I should also mention that my wife is a singularly attractive human being, and that I felt a strange pleasure sitting beside her on a stage in front of a crowd of people. I knew many of the men envied me.

On the night in question, both Claudia and I succumbed quite readily to the rhythmic swing of the pendulum and the soothing, relaxing voice of our friend. We were not the only subjects though. Three or four other persons had also volunteered. One volunteer in particular, Mr. Elmwood Anderson, who had been a colleague of mine years before I transferred to the Beinecke collection, sat on the right hand side of my wife. He had been making eyes at her all evening. I secretly hoped that Sherril would make an utter ass out of my pompous and amorously bloated friend.

As I recall it now, with a mind not entirely of my own, I was called upon to perform certain harmless stunts. Sherril had given me ample assurance that he would not stick needles through my palms nor torture me in any way. No, the stunts he called upon me to perform were quite simple and innocuous. He presented me with a lemon and told me that it was an apple. I devoured the lemon and found it delicious, not sour at all, but I have always been able to suck fresh lemons. It requires no special talent, I might add. It is a common hypnotic stunt and it pleases the vulgar. My friend next instructed me to gaze intently at the red stage curtain and to describe a painting that he said was hanging there. I knew there was no painting suspended on the curtain. Any fool with two good eyes could tell that, but I described a painting anyway. I had no desire not to. And, I must add, the crowd was treated to a very imaginative and sensuous description of colors, line, and shade. I suppose it is well known in our little circle that I might have been an art historian had I not married Claudia, but there is no need for me to explore that problem here. I was later informed by certain members of the audience that everyone had laughed uproariously when I leapt from my chair simply because Sherril had mentioned that it was on fire. I recall neither the chair feeling hot nor the audience making any outburst at. In fact, I should label the entire event, my part in it at least, a practical joke upon the audience if it were not for the more serious incident.

I do not know how long I remained in my state of lassitude, but as I have noted, I felt that I had complete control, felt that I could break his commands at any time. When I opened my eyes, I saw an auditorium of faces smiling at me. There was a feeling of warmth, a feeling of goodness permeating the auditorium, and so I smiled back. I must say I did feel quite relaxed and quite refreshed. I had closed my eyes for only a few minutes, but I felt as if I had been sleeping solidly for eight hours. I was even infused with a sense of forgiveness for my old colleague Mr. Anderson.

My wife and the others were soon brought out—that I hasten to add is Sherril's term and not mine—but neither my wife nor I felt any urge to depart from the stage. In fact it felt good to be in the limelight for a change. Also, my wife was now on the downstage left side of the stage. She had started the experiment by sitting next to me and I must admit that I was puzzled by the change. What had she been doing on the downstage left side of the stage? I looked at her and smiled and she returned the smile. At this moment she appeared very radiant and strikingly tall in her high-heel shoes.

I stood up and crossed the stage, preparing to take my wife's arm so that we might walk down the steps together, but as soon as I approached her, her smile disappeared. She leaped away from me, her hands to her face. "Help, help me," she shrieked at me with unspeakable horror. "Get that beast away from me!" I immediately whirled around—was there an animal behind me that was frightening my wife so? But there was no animal. There was only Sherril smirking at me, and the other volunteers, along with members of the audience, were laughing and laughing. As I turned back to my wife, I could see that Claudia was frozen in a state of panic. She was trembling from head to toe, and tears were flowing freely down her face. I reached out for her to comfort her, but she shrieked again and collapsed to the floor. The audience by now was frozen into silence, for it was now plain to any but the most blithering idiot that my wife was experiencing a fit, a bout of hysteria. The closer I came to her, the worse she became. Her breath was coming in short spurts and her body movements were agitated and spastic. "Stay back you fool," Sherril cried, pushing me to one side. "Don't touch her."

I growled a reply, or if it wasn't a growl it should have been, for I was now suspended between fear for my wife and complete befuddlement. I turned toward the audience for help, but all I could see were people standing up on their chairs to get a better view. I felt very heavy, overweight and ponderous. My nerves were raw and were not helped at all by Elmwood Anderson's hyena-like outbursts. He and another volunteer were holding onto my arms and trying to prevent me from reaching my wife.

"She'll be all right," Sherril explained. "It's just a post-hypnotic suggestion that has gotten a little out of hand."

"She thinks you're a gorilla!" somebody yelled, and I nodded in agreement as if it were the most natural explanation in the world. My shirt was soaked through for I was sweating profusely, a sweating brought on by both anxiety and by the incredibly hot stage lights. I remember finding a certain satisfaction in noting that on the stage border lights, blue bulbs were placed in every fourth position.

"Can't you see that she's terrified of you?" Sherril asked, raising my wife's head slightly and applying a bottle of smelling salts to her nostrils. "Go sit down," Sherril commanded, a command he followed quickly by an appeal to the audience, "Is there a doctor in the house? Is there a doctor in the house?" It seemed that if there were a doctor in the house, he would have been on stage by now; I knew that Claudia should soon be recovered, and so I was only bothered by a terrible hunger. I would have eaten anything. I returned to my chair and sat there scratching my head.

"Hey King Kong, want a banana?" some kid yelled, but I tried not to pay any attention.

Twenty or twenty-five minutes later an ambulance arrived and my wife was carried off on a stretcher. She had revived, but Sherril had been careful not to move her. There was a doctor on the stage, but I didn't like him. I didn't like his officious attitude, but I didn't say anything. I know I should have accompanied Claudia to the hospital. In fact, I wanted to accompany Claudia in the ambulance, but Sherril advised against it. He said that the post-hypnotic suggestion had not been removed from her mind, and that if she saw me again she would only suffer another bout of hysteria. I agreed with him. It made very clear sense to me.

After most of the people had been cleared from the auditorium, Sherril sat on a chair beside me, wiping his brow with a handkerchief. "You see," Sherril told me, nervously pondering every word, as indeed he might since it was his idea that Claudia and I be involved in his experiment in the first place. "You see," Sherril repeated, looking out over the empty seats, not daring to look me in the eye, "right before I brought you and Claudia out of your sleep, I planted a post-hypnotic suggestion in Claudia's mind. I told her that when you stood up from your chair and crossed the stage that she would see you as a gorilla. In your mind I planted the suggestion that you were to move with gorilla-like movements. As I hope you understand, I had no idea that Claudia would react so strongly."

I didn't say anything. What could I say?

"Obviously my suggestion was in poor taste, and I can only offer my most humble apologies and my promise that as soon as possible I shall hypnotize her and remove the horrible suggestion from her mind." Sherril squeezed his hands together and glanced nervously at the floor. He had gulped many of his words so I could not be completely sure that I had heard him correctly. But I refused to act in haste or in desperation. If I murdered him for his lack of taste, his lack of sense, his lack of propriety, I might not ever get my wife back. I needed Sherril so that he could remove, as promised, the post-hypnotic suggestion from Claudia's mind. Still, I did not deign to answer him. He was not worthy of reply. He was not worthy to be breathing the same air I was breathing; he was not worthy to be sitting on the same stage with me. I stood up from my chair and crossed the stage slowly, walking heavily through the aisle of the auditorium. There was still a great hunger in the pit of my stomach. I walked all the way home since I was obviously in no condition to drive.

For two days, I moped about the house, not at all knowing what to do. Of course I had called the hospital at the first opportunity, but had been informed that my wife had been released only a few hours after entering. Sherril had brought her to his house and had stopped by to pick up some of her clothes. I attempted to speak with Claudia by phone, but even the sound of my voice severely disturbed her. According to Sherril, who had to act as an interpreter of sorts, it made my wife sick to her stomach just to envision me as a large hairy gorilla standing in the middle of the living room with a small black telephone in my paw. Sherril and I attempted to reassure her that I was the same loving husband I had always been, but it was to no avail. Sherril still informed me that it was useless for me to do anything at all. "All you can do," Sherril explained, "is stay out of Claudia's sight until I put her under hypnosis again."

Naturally I have repeatedly implored him to begin his remedy as soon as possible, but he informs me that Claudia is resisting his efforts to place her under hypnosis. "This is understandable," he has said in his most recent letter from Paris—he believes that travel will aid Claudia and will cause her to be more relaxed—"because of the traumatic experience she has undergone. We're going to have to give her more time." I, of course, am footing the bills. I will spare no expense to make her well.

"More time." No one can possibly imagine the bitterness those words hold for me. I have been without Claudia for almost three months now, and I am beginning to lose hope. I sit in my favorite easy chair, staring at the walls, or I pace back and forth in the rooms my wife and I once shared together. When I can concentrate, I study books on hypnosis in the hope that I will strike upon a clue to relieve Claudia's mind of its terrible delusion. The most logical possibility seems to be shock therapy, for this is in keeping with A. K. Dickerson's theory, as published in *The Philosophy of Mesmerism, or Animal Magnetism,* that, "We know we are surrounded by an infinitely thin, elastic, volatile fluid, that we inspire and expire it every moment of our life, but the component parts, the inherent qualities, no one can determine whether it be electricity or galvanism beyond our realm." If it is not beyond our realm, perhaps Claudia's volatile fluid would be susceptible to electric shock. Sherril, however, insists that I am misreading Dickerson. He writes me that the volatile fluid is much too sensitive to be tampered with by anyone but by the original hypnotist.

When my friend and my wife return from Paris, I will demand that he act upon my idea. In the meantime, I take some comfort in knowing that my wife and I are quite happily married and that we will soon resume our tranquil relationship, just as soon as Sherril can effect a cure. Poor Sherril. It must be a terrible burden on him to assume the moral responsibility of this catastrophe and to have for a house-guest a woman who is not completely in her right mind and one who has been, in the recent past, not very friendly toward him. Well, all three of us must be more patient. It is difficult for me though, for, knowing how my handwriting upsets Claudia, he has forbidden me to write her.

Jazz City

⟋⟍

Look, you want to know how to lose? I know more ways of losing than the next man. The other morning, for example, I had $500 to win on a horse named Jazz City and it came in. Did it pay off? Not on your tintype. Why? Because of a mechanical malfunction on the tout board.

Such are the ways of Destiny.

SECOND—$14.000. 3-up. Cl ($50-45,000) 6 f Off 1;57 time 22¼

Horses	Wt.	PP	¼	½	str.	Fin.	jockey
4-Jazz City	114	2	1	2	1¾	1½	Bailey
1-Weigh the Gold	114	1	4	7	2¼	2 6	Ferret
9-1-inville Ridge	109	4	3	3	3¾	3	Martinez
Glorious Fool	114	5	6	6½	5	4½	Romero
Jumping Jamie	114	7	5	2	5¾	5	Migliore
Flawless Stone	114	8	2	4	6	6½	Thibeau
Sassy Note	114	3	7	7	7	7	Cordero
Orion's Sword	114	4	4	8	8	8	McCauley

Scr.-Wavering Moon (I), Forlions Cover (0), Lion Sleeps (E), pr. Red (A), John Regent (M), Climate Zone (Cg), Chemical Warfare (H), Postal Strike (P), Merry Mixer (Q), Skate Gently (R), Binny

(S), Hail the Brave (T). Consolation Double (C-All horses 2d race) paid $3.40. OTB-Consolation Double-$3.20 This race was run for purse money only due to tout-board malfunction.

I only bring the above matter up so you will understand why I was in such a miserable mood when my son brought home his report card with only a B– in Pain.

"How could you do that?" I shouted at him. "Don't you hurt like the rest of us?"

THE REST OF THIS PAGE IS BLANK IN CONFORMITY TO THE PAPER LIBERALIZATION ACT

Reader is free to write comments here.

We want your eyes down here.

"I guess not, Pop," he said, taking up his fourth-baseman's glove and absquatulating from the house. Poor kid. He's only twelve. How can he possibly know how important good grades are. Rojah did, however, score an 88 in Firearms, and a more than respectable 93.5 in

Empathy with the Lower Classes, among whom—because of my status as an Internal Huntsman—he counts himself.

Since the boy's mother had long ago run off with the family fortune, it was incumbent upon my broad shoulder or shoulders (on those days when I have more than one) to meet with his teacher—an uncertain redhead named Marybeth 414 Pruett—a 6th-Form Fascist representing the Philadelphia Normal School.

"How can my boy get only a B– in Pain?" I asked her, after I had removed my tweed hat and squeezed into one of the tiny desks. I believe the real reason teachers request meetings with parents (or as more than likely these days—with the single parent) is that they derive great joy watching grown men, such as myself, trying to accommodate their bulk (I'm six-foot-two and weigh 223 pounds) into desks designed for amoebas. Persons who work as Internal Huntsmen tend not to be small. We have too many large animals to transport from place to place. "He hurts as much as anyone," I told her. I grinned. "Of course you may ask me how much does anyone hurt?" I added. Perhaps, if I turned on the charm, I could seduce her, take her on her chalk-filled desk, her panties tossed over the blades of the overhead fan, her shaved legs in the air, the bottoms of her white shoes brushing against the American flag. Oh say can you see. . . .

"38.6 is average these days," she said, not noticing my charm, or pretending not to.

"Well, I know that," I said, "but my son is above average."

"A is above average, Mr. Murobyne." She opened her desk and removed a manila folder containing print-outs of Rojah's life-work. Probably contained my life-work as well. If my own desk had been somewhat bigger I would have squirmed. Every clean thought had absquatulated from my brain. Only the most vile and filthy jokes came to mind, the kind of jokes only an Internal Huntsman would have access to after his clients have made their kill and have celebrated long into the night with bootleg liquor. Some hunters, those jokers.

"You busted his knee-cap on Thursday," I told her. "Certainly you must have given him extra credit for a busted knee-cap."

She shook her head. Her face, framed as was by a curly mane of uncertain red hair, was covered with freckles. Her teeth were as white and as straight as I had ever seen. "If your son had just spoken out or even if he had said something, I might have been able to raise his grade. But he just sat there. Even when we're rupturing his spleen, he refuses to give an oral report."

"What's he supposed to say? That it hurts like hell?"

Ms. Pruett shook her head. I thought maybe I should unzip my fly and offer her some extra credit of my own, but she looked like the kind of woman who would have none of it. But, then, I was well-acquainted with her husband. I couldn't really blame her for taking up public school teaching in all its glory.

"Rojah, when he's in pain, *if* he's in pain, could say what the others say."

"And what's that?" I asked, pretending to be interested. In reality, all I cared about was getting her to change the grade so Rojah would have a better chance of joining the Institute for Political Networking. Hardly anyone in there had less than straight A's.

"How much he wants to succeed."

I nodded. Like father like son. Always running away from success, betting on some winning horse only to have it disqualified.

"But there is some hope, Mr. Murobyne," she said, rapidly turning over the papers in the files. "He was nearly perfect in Levitation."

"But it's only Levitation," I said. "No one takes Levitation seriously."

"I do."

Her answer placed me in such an awkward position that I could only swallow hard. "It's pretty to look at, but it's not as important as Pain."

"I think all the subjects here are equally important." Her face was hardening into a permanent scowl. "Maybe your son is trying too hard. Perhaps Rojah needs a hobby."

"He has a hobby."

"Oh?" I don't think she quite believed me.

"Monetary cut-outs. He snips the pictures of the Presidents from paper money and pastes them into scrapbooks."

Ms. 414 Pruett's mouth dropped open and I thought of one or three things I could have popped into it. She knew I was lying. "Perhaps you could ask him to bring his scrapbooks in and share them with his classmates. It's always refreshing when students discover outside interests." She looked at her watch. I had overstayed my welcome.

"Look, Ms. Pruett," I said, trying to extricate myself from the tiny desk, "I know Sir Pruett."

"You do?"

"Yes, and I know how much your husband loves to hunt. Suppose I brought him a caribou this afternoon. I think he would enjoy the opportunity of killing a caribou. Why don't you call him and tell him that I'll bring one by your apartment by five o'clock."

She leaned her chin onto her hands. Her white elbows were resting on a stack of Levitation books. She fluttered her eyelids ever so briefly. "And why would you want to do that for Cos, Mr. Murobyne?"

THE PREVIOUS PAGE IS REPEATED TO CONFORM TO THE PAGE REPETITION ACT

"He has a hobby."

"Oh?" I don't think she quite believed me.

"Monetary cut-outs. He snips the pictures of the Presidents from paper money and pastes them into scrapbooks."

Ms. 414 Pruett's mouth dropped open and I thought of one or three things I could have popped into it. She knew I was lying. "Perhaps you could ask him to bring his scrapbooks in and share them with his classmates. It's always refreshing when students discover outside interests." She looked at her watch. I had overstayed my welcome.

"Look, Ms. Pruett," I said, trying to extricate myself from the tiny desk, "I know Sir Pruett."

"You do?"

"Yes, and I know how much your husband loves to hunt. Suppose I brought him a caribou this afternoon. I think he would enjoy the opportunity of killing a caribou. Why don't you call him and tell him that I'll bring one by your apartment by five o'clock."

She leaned her chin onto her hands. Her white elbows were resting on a stack of Levitation books. She fluttered her eyelids ever so briefly. "And why would you want to do that for Cos, Mr. Murobyne?"

PAGE 50 IS REPEATED TO CONFORM TO THE PAGE-REPETITION ACT

Because, you silly bitch, I thought, I want you to change my son's grade to an A. "Because you've been so understanding about Rojah's plight," I said. I should have laughed in my sleeve. "I think I should return the favor. Go ahead. You call him. Tell him I'm on the way there. It'll be his chance of a lifetime." I pushed my hat onto my head and made my escape. *Escape—A+.*

On the street I thought that it was time to move on. Everything was falling apart. The music of the spheres was off-key. I thought how a stranger could enter your house at any time and say, "I want your children or your eyes," and there would be very little you could do about it. Vicious strangers were tossing bottles out of windows and there wasn't any time to duck. No wonder the sportspersons were staying home.

I walked directly to the Internal Huntsman Offices, filled out the necessary vouchers, and procured the caribou for Ms. Fascist's husband.

Ms. 414 Pruett, since she did not rise to my oh-say-can-you-see bait, most likely decided that I would go back on my word and leave her husband high, wide, and stranded; but I was nothing if I was not a man of my word. And I wasn't really a man of my word.

I drove the caribou across town and unloaded it. The most difficult part of my job is getting my animals to and from the truck. That's because people always stop to stare. Sometimes, because they're so vicious, they even throw objects at the animals. It's then I have license to kill. I can't even begin to tell you how much living in the city is getting to me.

THE FOLLOWING PAGES ARE SUBJECT TO READER JUSTIFICATION TAX

I must confess that, although I had met Cos Pruett on several occasions, I had never been to his apartment before. I was, thus, pleasantly surprised how well appointed it was. Chintz furniture. Several large paintings of barometers and other scientific apparatus. An antique dining table under a splendid chandelier. I knew he had inherited his wealth, but I also knew that, like the rest of us, he was dying of boredom. Perhaps that was the true reason his red-haired wife had retreated to spleen-bursting.

"I liked the old days much better," Mr. Pruett said, after the butler had chauffered me in. Or after the Chauffeur had butlered me in. One or the other.

I shrugged. Mr. Pruett, dressed in his tweed hunting jacket, poured me some bootleg bourbon. It was strong, but I paid it no compliment. I was determined not to be impressed. On numerous occasions I had delivered big game to the wealthy. I had stood inside the hallways and master bedrooms of the richest people in the world. It was just another job, more or less.

"In the old days, we could go outside and do our hunting," Mr. Pruett continued, "but now it's much too dangerous."

"Yes," I told him.

"I don't know how you do it, coming all the way over here in broad daylight. I don't have that kind of courage anymore."

"I have a kid in school," I said, finishing the bourbon. "And I have to pay rent."

That final phrase must have surprised him, for his head snapped back and his eyes opened wide. "Yes," he said after a while. "I guess you must."

Why Marybeth 414 would have married such a snob, such an old codger (I guessed his age to be late 60's or early 70's) was beyond me, though I assume some women are impressed with any man with a title. *Sir* Pruett I should have called him. But I didn't. Wouldn't. Couldn't.

Mr. Pruett clapped his hands. "Well, let's get started."

The rules for Internal Hunting were much the same for every borough. There weren't any. I delivered the game and stayed out of the way as much as I could. If the apartment were particularly large, and if the animal were not over-drugged and were sufficiently spirited, enough expensive furniture would topple to provide me with some amusement.

Most of the time, especially if I was at the end of my day, I would sit in the library and browse through magazines, waiting for the ordeal to be over. The worst part was the mess afterward. All that blood on walls and floors and furniture. It could almost turn me against the sport.

(Sir) Pruett had amassed an extensive collection of guns and rifles, but then so had almost everyone else in the city. Guns were easy to come by. Good huntsmen were not. On a scale of one to ten, I had rated Cosgrove a six, perhaps a seven. He wasn't too bad. He had killed them all! The Eland. The Zebra. The Hippopotamus. The Rhinoceros. The Snipe. The Elephant. Who could blame him if today his mouth watered at the sight of a slightly naked caribou frolicking in his living-room.

Cos took down a 1905 Deer Stalker and an 1897 303 Bristol Boss. The Boss had been made by a certain Charles Lancaster of London. It amused some of the wealthy to hunt with antiques. It added to the fun, though I personally knew of one hunter who saw his antique punt gun misfire and, instead of bringing down the black bear I had delivered, had sprayed pellets into the forehead of one of his servants. Not that it mattered. Huntsmen were allowed points for servants. We merely severed the head from the body (for mounting purposes) and disposed of the rest in a garbage bag. At the end of a day, it was not uncommon to see the streets of the city lined with body bags. A common children's game was to bet money on the sex of the victim.

"You wish to join me?" Mr. Pruett asked.

I shook my head. He was merely being polite. There was no way he was going to allow an Internal Huntsman upstage his sport. "No, thanks. I'll wait here. Just call me when you're done." And, I thought, assure me that Rojah's grade is going to be changed to an A.

He nodded and went out, closing the door behind him. I leapt for the bourbon, promising to do as much damage to it as I could. Most of the hunts took considerable time because it was a luxury, like good bourbon, to be savored. Oftentimes the hunters would set up a series of mirrors and try trick shots, while their game leapt over sofas and love-seats or attempted to ram their horns through television sets.

I, myself, was most fond of the American Elk (*Cervus canadensis*)—the structure of its horns, the extreme cleft of its hooves, and the short tail, almost like the scut of a hare. No matter how you looked at the situation, Sir Pruett owed me one. Next time I would just bring some ducks and toss them into the swimming pool.

There were several shots. Then quiet. The door opened, and Pruett, followed by his butler/chauffeur who was carrying the rifles, staggered in. His hunting vest was smeared with blood.

"I finished him off with this," he said, proudly displaying a bread knife. "The devil had made a mad dash for the bathroom, but I finally cornered him in the kitchen. Good show. Good show." He held out his other hand and I placed a glass of bourbon in it. Then I followed the butler/chauffeur/servant/slave/underling into the kitchen to assist with the cleaning up. That was the part of the job I despised the most. At about six-thirty, or so, Marybeth returned, but she barely acknowledged my presence and said nothing at all about my son.

After Sir Pruett finished signing all the forms—that's my job mostly, keeping track of copies and copies of forms—I bagged the headless animal and dragged it down to my truck. Another day of sport well done. The things a parent will do to help his child to succeed in the world, whatever world it was, to whomever it belonged.

At home, Rojah greeted me at the door with a great red blotch on his neck. He was weeping.

"What's the matter?" I asked.

"They tried to hang me," he blurted out, throwing his arms around my waist. With him hanging on, I managed to get inside and pull the door shut.

I threw the bolt for the deadlock.

"Who?" I asked.

"My friends. They said they needed extra credit for Hanging."

"And you? I suppose you don't," I said, plopping myself onto the sofa and wondering who would make supper. I oftentimes had made stews from the left-over carcasses, but tonight I was too tired to deal with it. That's the real reason kids are the way they are today. Parents are just too tired to deal with things. "Maybe you would do better if you applied yourself more."

I would have turned on some arcade games, but my wife had also absqualated with the video games, and I, with my hectic schedule, couldn't find the time to replace them. Garbagehead XlHs Maestro was our favorite.

"Can I take Hanging next semester?" Rojah asked. He was on the sofa with me, his head on my lap. Poor kid. I knew how he felt. Always to be left out of things. "We'll see," I told him. "We'll see. In the meantime, I want you to drop Pain. That course is for losers."

"Maybe Mrs. Pruett will change her mind and give me an A."

"I don't think so," I said. "She wants you to talk more in class. She wants you to say things about the things she's teaching you."

"When they put the pins under my eyelids, I did all right," he said, drifting off into sleep. "An 85 plus." Poor kid. He had been crying a long time, so I let him fall asleep. My own education had not been quite so rigorous. I think my best course had been Reincarnation of Mad Historical Figures. There had been a lot of them. And they killed a lot of people.

Jazz City, I thought. I wanted to get out, move to somewhere safer, someplace where strangers wouldn't come at you with baseball bats, hammer you to the ground, and leave you a vegetable for the rest of your life. Somewhere where strangers wouldn't break into your apartment, say, "Your eyes or your children," and leave you bleeding on the carpet. Alas!

The more I thought about it, the more I realized there was nowhere else to go. Escape routes were closing down. No pretty music.

My son and I must have remained on the darkened sofa for more than an hour. I kept waiting for the phone to ring. Mrs. Pruett with her token to the Promised Land. But, of course, she didn't call. The rich are never grateful when you do them a favor. Favors are what they expect.

I hummed the National "Ode to Death" and patted my son's head and wondered what he was dreaming.

THE END

Alternate endings are available through the Alternate-Ending Bureau of the Committee to Avoid Boredom in the Classics. You may write them directly or call them in on the toll-free hotline.

We want your eyes down here.

John Locke and His Bicycle

Since Dr. Albert T. Flax has surrendered himself to the police, there really is no mystery to solve. I must confess, however, that not since The Case of the Tap Dancing Beggar, have I—the Reverend Michael Poe of Falmouth's Unitarian Church—ever been so perplexed, amused, and dismayed by the welter of critical comment that has surrounded . . . well, shall I label it The Case of John Locke's Bicycle?

The tragic story of Dr. Flax, late of Trinity College, and his absolute devotion to the life and thought of the philosopher John Locke, is of course well-known to the academic community, especially to the colleges of Cambridge and Oxford, where Professor Flax's name and deeds have been bandied about like a shuttlecock. So much gossip, rumor, and misinterpretation of events—all communicated with little regard for the feelings of the surviving members of the family. Thus, though the story is popular among scholars, it has not received wide play in the popular press, I trust it will not be a complete waste of time to recount it here, to add it to my accounts of local crime and to the general history of scandal that so illuminates the blackened heart of the modern world.

ITEM: Dr. Albert Flax, Age 50, Full Professor of Philosophy at Trinity College, met his wife one spring morning while she was riding her bicycle across campus. Dr. Flax was walking, with head down, his white hair blowing in the wind, his gown flapping, his thought thoroughly engrossed upon some problem in logic, when Trudy Fairbaugh, aged 23, a light-skinned slender beauty, nearly plowed her bicycle into the learned professor. He fell to the ground with a thud. So did the lovely Miss Fairbaugh. It was love at first sight. For both of them. They were married in my church on a fine Sunday morning about four years ago. Their marriage, perhaps because of the discrepancy of some 30 years in their ages, was not a happy one, I am sad to say.

ITEM: The following letter was sent to me by Professor Flax some six to seven months after his initial meeting with Ms. Fairbaugh. Though it is a long letter (the Professor, during his bachelor years, had fallen into the habit of writing lengthy epistles to neighboring clergy), permit me to quote it in its entirety, for the Professor's letter presents the more pertinent details of the case:

*August 17, 19_*

My Dear Reverend Poe:

I am writing you this evening in the flush of excitement. A literary detective has never entered upon such a series of important discoveries.

I must share with you a recent literary goldmine that has fallen, so to speak, into my academic purview: a hitherto unpublished manuscript by John Locke, a manuscript in which that great philosopher examines in detail Mankind's indebtedness to the bicycle as a vehicle for human understanding. This 450-page manuscript has been languishing for nearly 300 years in the back offices of Lancaster and Robbins, two solicitors who occupied five sparsely furnished rooms at 26 S Marlin's Lane, London.

Had my aunt not been a close friend (and possibly mistress) to Sylvester Lancaster, the papers might never have fallen to me.

The turn of events is indeed a happy accident. Perhaps the same observation might be made about my wife—it too was only a happy accident that she fell to me, actually on me—but I shall not burden the sophisticated reader (among whom I count you one) with obvious par-

*allelisms that exist between philosophy and myself. Life consists of par-
allel lines. It is a miracle when anything meets at all*

*About the Locke Manuscript (hereafter abbreviated LM): My col-
leagues warn me that I am being duped, my career placed in jeopardy
by some malicious prankster, some part-time instructor disgruntled by
the prerogatives of senior professors, some academic underling seething
with bitterness and rancor, some all-but-doctorate overburdened with
illiterate themes—but allow me to state that there is no longer any doubt
in my mind, nor in the minds of my relatives, nor in the minds of our
nation's leading Locke scholars (whose names are so well-known that I
need not list them here) that the recently discovered LM (by myself) is
indeed genuine. The handwriting has been scrutinized. Experts agree: It
is written in John Locke's hand. The ink and manuscript papers have
been chemically analyzed and carbon-dated They belong to the proper
century. Let there be no question in anyone's mind that the LM is genuine. Let there be no question about that!*

*If I may be so bold; I should beg you to consider the LM as the UR-
ESSAY CONCERNING HUMAN UNDERSTANDING.*

*When John Locke took up his pen, he began his career by inventing
the bicycle. He became enamoured of the work of his own hand and
brain and set forth his ideas about the vehicle in a monumental work
entitled "An Essay Concerning the Bicycle." Later, when he had completed a first draft and when it finally dawned upon his seething brain
that he was so far ahead of his times—indeed it was a century when it
seemed that everybody was ahead of his or her time—that the ungainly
philosopher realized that he would be hooted at in the streets, that doors
would slam in his face, that his university career would be nipped in the
bud, that he would become the laughing stock of an entire generation.
And so he suffered a complete breakdown. He tossed the original LM
into a child's trunk, placed the trunk onto a wheelbarrow, and trundled
the manuscript off to the offices of his solicitors, Lancaster and Robbins.
There, for centuries, the LM remained, gathering dust, and safe from
prying eyes and impertinent inquiries.*

Of course I realize that I may be opening my own career to ridicule by revealing the content of that child's trunk, but, my dear Reverend, you must realise that truth, in whatever form it takes, no matter how ludicrous, must be served My erstwhile colleagues (and nothing is more erstwhile than a colleague in a Department of Philosophy) may sit apart from me and mock my endeavors; they may push their trays of envy across the cafeteria of time; but they shall not stay this courier from his route.

So much for the preamble. Now for the juice!

I shall quote directly from the work in question. Book 14 Chapter 4 of the LM: "God having designed man for a sociable creature, made him not only with an inclination, and under a necessity to have fellowship with those of his own kind; but furnished him also with the bicycle, which is to be the great instrument and common tie of society.

"First, mankind assumes that their bicycles be marks of success in the minds of other men with whom they (the men) communicate.

"Second, bicycles, by long and familiar use, come to excite in men and in women certain ideas so constantly and readily that they are apt to suppose a natural connection between the mode of transportation used and the kind of ideas that spring to mind. On foot, we think one way; on a bicycle, another."

Here the manuscript breaks off and the philosopher plunges into a wealth of considerations about Modes of Pleasure and Pain and the influence the bicycle has had upon such modes. (The chapter on Bicycles and their Origins is, alas, terribly inept, for Mr. Locke presumably lacked the patience of the historian. Research in dusty archives where he could have uncovered working models of the vehicle was not for him). Once again I quote from materials to be published in the Oxford edition: "A bicycle is a delight of the mind, We are in possession of any bicycle, when we have it so in our power that we can use it when we please. Lack of a bicycle causes uneasiness in the mind."

The thought of losing one's bicycle, which might have been enjoyed longer, introduces further unease. Despair is the thought of the unattain-

ableness of any bicycle, and Envy is an uneasiness of the mind caused by the consideration of someone else's bicycle, a bicycle obtained by one we think should not have had it before us.

A bicycle, whether in motion or lying still at rest, is not by anyone taken to be a free agent. If we inquire into the reason, we shall find it is because we conceive not a bicycle to think and consequently not to have any volition, or preference for motion over rest, or vice versa; and therefore a bicycle has not liberty, is not a free agent; but all its motion and rest come under our idea of necessary, and are so called. Although I could multiply infinitely (not quite infinitely, of course—I was merely adding a touch of humor to an almost humorless discussion), I believe I have made my point. Once my presentation of this material is made to the scholarly world, I shall be able to raise enough foundation and grant money to take my beloved wife for a trip around the world, that trip she has always longed for.

Sincerely yours,
ATF

Needless to say, I read and reread the above epistle with considerable anxiety. I had not studied the writings of John Locke in over two decades, but there was certainly no mention of the invention of the bicycle in any of the materials I had read. Or could the Professor be right? Locke had, of course, treated the real and fantastical side of things. Professor Flax, perhaps, had fallen onto the fantastical side of things.

The following morning I myself bicycled to the Professor's house and was astonished to find it shuttered and locked. Neither the Professor nor his attractive young wife was to be seen. Neighbors felt that for some reason, perhaps the nonpayment of debts, they had shot the moon. I made no mention to anyone of the letter in my possession.

ITEM: How the marriage of Dr. Flax ran into considerable difficulties. This knowledge comes to me by the way of Douglas

MacDonald, who tends the bar at the White Horse Pub. One morning, Dr. Flax had placed his beloved wife onto the train to Dover, and, to help assuage his grief at the loneliness brought upon him by the necessity of wife's travel (a trip brought on because of illness in his wife's family), he took himself to the Pub.

After two, perhaps three, Guinnesses, Dr. Flax struck up a conversation with a certain Albert Fraser, a man not completely unknown to followers of the Polo Circuit. "Had to put my wife on the train this morning," Mr. Fraser said, standing outside the Pub with Dr. Flax at his elbow.

"That so?" said Dr. Flax.

"Yessir. Had to send my wife to Dover."

"Dover, is it?"

"Yes, Dover."

Dr. Flax considered the news. Sipped his Guinness. Watched the August sun climbing high into the sky.

"A coincidence, Sir," he finally blurted out.

"A coincidence?" asked Mr. Fraser.

"Why yes."

"What coincidence?" asked Mr. Fraser. Attired in his polo costume, Mr. Fraser placer his whip under his left arm and struck a formal pose in the sunlight. The train carrying Trudy Fairbaugh was somewhere in limbo, chugging along peacefully between Falmouth and Dover.

"I, too, this very morning have placed my wife upon the train to Dover," the Professor explained, shaking his head at the strangeness of the world.

"Ah!" The polo player sipped his ale and nodded his head. It was difficult to say whether the exclamation applied to Fraser's approval of the drink or if it were his timely response to the notion of coincidence.

"Well, perhaps our wives will meet this day, as you and I have done," Mr. Fraser said. "I am Albert Fraser." He extended his hand.

Dr. Flax took it. "Oh, yes, I know," the Professor said. "I have seen you play a number of times. I am Dr. Albert Flax."

"Pleased."

"Flattered."

"My wife is going down to visit her relative. Her mother is, unfortunately, quite ill."

"Say, isn't that something!" the professor exclaimed. "My wife's mother is also ailing."

"Extraordinary."

"Isn't it?"

"I can't wait until I tell Trudy," Fraser said. He balanced his glass on the wide ledge under the window. "Well, I must be off."

"Trudy? My wife's name is also Trudy."

"No."

"Yes."

After a moment of embarrassed silence, the Professor added: "Trudy Fairbaugh was her maiden name."

Fraser stopped dead in his tracks. The Professor nodded. He reached into his coat pocket and from his wallet extracted a recent snapshot. Fraser blanched. "Why . . . Why . . . Why. . . ." His voice broke.

The Professor turned beet red. "She doesn't have a twin sister by any chance?"

The Professor was in no condition to answer. The two men retreated inside, found a table away from the others, and compared notes. "I feel like an absolute fool," Fraser concluded.

"I know exactly what you mean."

The two men decided to drive directly to Dover and confront their wife-in-common directly.

ITEM: Noted Polo Star Found Dead on Dover Turnpike. From *The Guardian*: Albert Fraser, age 46, was found this morning on the Dover Turnpike, less than a mile from Exit 42A. Mr. Fraser, the well-known polo player, apparently had been hit by an automobile, the tragic victim of a hit-and-run accident.

ITEM: From the time-table that I have been able to piece together of the events, the discovery of the John Locke manuscripts must have occurred within two or three days after the untimely demise of Albert Fraser.

ITEM: Less than one week after the newspapers reported the death of the polo player, Trudy Fairbaugh-Flax-Fraser was found murdered on a bicycle path not far from the Northumberland Hotel. Mrs. Fairbaugh-Flax-Fraser's skull had been bashed in by a bicycle pump. Her own Peugeot Racer was found completely mangled, as if some giant had jumped up and down upon it. It was at that hotel that Professor Albert Flax and Trudy had registered under the names of Mr. and Mrs. Jeremiah Key. I presume that one man's key is another man's Locke. It was from the Northumberland Hotel that the good Professor Flax wrote what turned out to be his final epistle as a free man:

My Dear Reverend Poe:

My dear Trudy and myself have ventured to this hotel for a few days of rest and relaxation. Unfortunately, I cannot take my mind off John Locke's obsession with bicycles. While Trudy amuses herself by going off on long rides or on pleasant walks through the woodlands (always with the requisite bird book in her hand and the even more requisite pair of binoculars about her neck), I remain behind in our spacious rooms and study the manuscript that God has placed under my stewardship. Each day I awake with more excitement than the previous one. In the pages I have sent you, I noticed several errata. I hope you will forgive me if I present to you my corrections:

p. 65: Bicycles may be imprinted upon the mind; for a man may live and die at last in ignorance of what the true significance of a bicycle is.

p. 69: Every drowsy nod shakes their doctrine who teach that the soul is always thinking about bicycles.

p. 89: There are some bicycles that come into our minds by one sense only.

I hope that the above clarifies matters. Trudy sends her love.

Yours in haste,
ATF

What was particularly perplexing about the above letter is that it was written under the misguided notion that the Professor had shown me the entire Locke Manuscript. Indeed he had not. As of the present writing, I have only knowledge of it as presented to me by references in two letters, and in a stray piece of paper that I came across about a week ago when I happened to enter Professor Flax's house, still shuttered and beginning to take on the dankness of disuse, to retrieve some toilet articles that he requested I bring to the prison. On his bedroom bureau, enlivened with a full-colored portrait of his beloved wife seated on her bicycle, was a single sheet of paper. The paper appeared as if it had been torn from a notebook or diary. The paper read:

Many children, imputing the pain they endured at school by their instructors forcing them to ride bicycles, soon develop an aversion to that marvelous creation. They are never reconciled to the bicycle and they refuse to use one all their lives after. Thus, riding a bicycle becomes a torment to them, which otherwise possibly they might have made the great pleasure of their lives.

Although I had no right to the document, I helped myself to it. I am keeping it in a safe place, awaiting the arrival of the official edition that the Professor insists will be issued by Oxford Press. I myself have yet to see any announcement of such a book in the literary columns of the *Times*. Perhaps because of the lurid circumstances surrounding the discovery of the material, the manuscript is being suppressed? These days, who can tell?

As for the fate of Professor Flax: the poor man has been sentenced to be hanged, an execution that will be carried out within the fortnight. Professor Flax has spoken to me about his tombstone. He should like it to read:

Hic juxt situs est Albertus Flax. Si qualis fuerit rogas, mediocritate sua contentum se vixisse respondet. Literis innutritus eousque tantum profecit, ut veritati unice litaret. Hoc ex scriptis illius discce; quae quod de eo reliquum est majori fide tibi exhibebunt quam epitaphii suspecta elogia. Virtues, si quas habuit, minores sane quam quas sibi laudi tibi in exemplum proponeret. Vitia una sepeliantur. Morum exemplum si quaeras in Evangelio habes: bicycle. Mortumm Anno Dom. 19__. Oct. 28.

I am not certain how the authorities will take to such an elaborate monument to a wife-slayer and the murderer of a brilliant polo player, but I shall do my best upon Professor Flax's behalf. In any case, these are the facts that I have at my disposal. (Perhaps the Professor was correct: Life consists only of parallel lines.) I hope they shall prove to be of use to future historians and to all those who pursue the matter of John Locke's Bicycle.

On the Street of
the Mad Magicians

~~~

Many bad things can happen to an innocent in a strange hotel room with a woman who is not his wife. Such are the axioms that never get printed inside Chinese fortune cookies.

But I blundered forward. I ordered the necessary magical apparatus. I met my client's mistress. She was in her early twenties, red-haired, red hair in all the right places, and, most satisfactory for my purposes, small, somewhat under five feet, with narrow feet. Her name was Irma, a name not as common as it once was when *My Friend Irma* was a popular radio program (and didn't the Hal Wallis films introduce Dean Martin & Jerry Lewis to the screen?), and I must say that I liked her right away. She was strange, but no stranger than other people I had met. Indeed, I once knew a man who made his living slipping on bananas. He would drop a banana peel in the lobby of a tony building and, in front of witnesses, he'd take a slip on it, then threaten the building's owner with expensive lawsuits. He would make from $850 to several thousand dollars per spill. A peculiar way to make a living, but it worked for him.

Who understands human nature? Only persons who produce reality TV shows or shows involving winning money. Me? I'm just a bleeding heart liberal. When I see a person bleeding I rush up and shove money into their wounds. That is, when I *have* money. Most days I have no money at all. But I am way ahead of my story.

As for Irma, if you had met her, you would have liked her. She had a good sense of humor, and she didn't mind, while floating in mid-air, rehearsing for her big love scene. She came from Chicago, had a baby, and claimed she loved Mr. Lau, her permanent patron and my temporary one. I didn't believe her though. I had lived long enough to know there were a lot of unhappy women in the world. She had a trace of an Irish accent, and when she spoke, her words simply hung in the air with a lilt. She floated; her words floated; good fortune, less than a mile away, also floated within my reach.

"And so I am going to be lying in mid-air and Sammy is going to be doing it to me, while you look on?" She laughed. I poured her another cup of coffee. We began to share many breakfasts, lunches, and dinners.

"I could look away," I lied.

"It would be decent of you," she said, turning her face to the sunlight. Her face was covered with freckles. "Positively decent. Do you think that this is a first? Am I the first woman in the history of the world to be screwed while floating, not in water, but in air?"

My ears turned red. Bright red.

"Why, Scott, my sweetheart, you're blushing."

"It's your language," I said.

"Yes," she said, putting her coffee cup down. "It's always the language. Never the deed."

"Sometimes the deed," I said. And we went back to work. God, she was smart. And that's always a dangerous thing in a woman.

Was she falling in love with me? Was I falling in love with her? Could I stand idly by and watch her patron make love to her?

No. I would float her high out of reach. Float her to the moon and beyond where only I could touch her. And then her patron would threaten to kill me, or to have me killed. And then I would have to leave town, move away from Pearl Street. Move away from Ratatouille and his elephantine mother, with Irma, as my new and semi-nude assistant, floating from town to town, Mr. Lau in hot pursuit. Floating from one place to another is certainly much better than taking Greyhound.

Yes, I say, we are like falcons who hook our talons together and make love in mid-air. Is that not what we all hope for? Such are the predictions about my future, predictions not to be found anywhere but in a life of my own choosing. Or was it a choice at all?

If I had not met Bernard Ratatouille, if I had not been in the right place at the right time, if I had not been a magician, if I had not charmed Mr. Lau's mistress out of her pants . . . . *If*. So many strange ideas floating through us. Although I cannot prove it, because the pain does not easily go away, our lives are mostly fantasy. Some events make sense if only told backwards.

Most likely, you are too young to remember the notorious theft of a First Folio of Shakespeare's plays from Williams College, my alma mater, and how, four months later, it was mysteriously returned by some unnamed, unknown messenger, a messenger so mysterious that he merely deposited his package at the library desk and disappeared into air, thin air. Left so quickly no one could even describe him. Four men from Buffalo were indicted for the theft. A little bargaining got them free. All four were acquaintances of Bernard Ratatouille. Ratatouille, in fact, was the one who designed the duplicate folio for them, a fake cover nicely tooled in red Moroccan leather. When one of Ratatouille's partners posed as a visiting professor, the partner quietly substituted the copy for the real one. It was ingenious to say the least. But not from the College's point of view. Williams College, in fact, did what it could to keep the theft out of the papers. Librarians and college presidents seeking alumni support do not take the theft of a first folio lightly. No doubt someone low on the totem pole of responsibility had to take the heat. Heat rises but not when assigning blame.

From time to time, during the seven years I knew him, Ratatouille would trot out a scrapbook he kept about the theft and show it to me. Bernard was not fond of many things, but he was fond of keeping scrapbooks. Some desperate men hold on for dear life to any bit and piece of life they come in contact with.

Alas! Desperation is never beautiful. So many women have left me because I have been too desperate.

In truth, I did not like the man, and should you meet Bernard Ratatouille, you would not like him either. Broad-shouldered and about forty pounds overweight, with a thin layer of salt-and-pepper hair, he was perpetually red-faced. His wide forehead was dotted with freckles, and there was and a scar over his left eye. On police posters he would have been easy to spot.

When we lived in the same building, across the street from a school for victims of cerebral palsy, Bernard was in his early fifties, and he too had many problems. Physical ones and psychological ones. Most con artists do, though the deepest and more severe of Bernie's problems stemmed from the fact that he, at age eleven, had accidentally killed his brother.

Because I have an amateur's interest in psychology, I wonder why no one has ever done a study of adults who have killed at a young age, either accidentally or on purpose, one of their friends or one of their siblings. Perhaps such a study has been done and I have missed it. As I say, I am a merely an amateur in these matters. Ratatouille calls me "the professional amateur."

But it's true. At age eleven, Bernard shot and killed his nine-year-old brother because his brother had been suffering from a tooth-ache. "Quit moaning and complaining," he told his brother, "because I can't stand anymore."

Unfortunately, the younger brother couldn't make his pain to go away. The younger brother, David, moaned and groaned and cried. Bernard got up from the couch, went upstairs to his father's room, opened a bureau drawer where his father kept a revolver, and went back downstairs. "I can't stand this noise!" he shouted. Then he pulled the trigger. He shot David through the head. The tooth-ache was gone for good, and so were many other things. If there were any good parts to Ratatouille's personality, those good parts became buried in a landslide of confusion and guilt. The parents never recovered. The father turned to alcohol for comfort and ended up robbing liquor stores with the very same pistol that had been used to kill his son.

Ratatouille, out of guilt, became the caretaker for his mother.

Perhaps it is not *Believe It Or Not* material, but every word is true. How can we tell the real from the false? Is that not the essential problem of life? Or of dealing with politicians? Or is the essential problem: How does one life differ from any other?

Am I being too simplistic? I am, as I've noted, not a professional psychologist or philosopher. I am merely that professional amateur—Milano the Great. I took my stage name off a package of spaghetti. Just like God, I make things float. I make things vanish, although whatever vanishes usually reappears. I specialize in entertaining customers at bars. It is not easy to keep people, especially people in bars, entertained.

There are people who can let things go, and there are people who can't. Bernard Ratatouille held onto everything. Every person from his past. Every scrap of paper. Maybe he realized what a thin thread there was separating each of us from oblivion. Keeping one's press notices proves something, but God knows what.

He lived with his mother in a tiny four-room flat on Pearl Street.

I lived on the floor directly over him. His mother, in response to the great sorrows of her life, had put on so much weight that she could not leave her room under her own power. Once a year, Ratatouille would knock on my door and ask me to help him carry his old lady down four flights of stairs and put her in a car for a trip to church. Or to somewhere. Maybe to the cemetery. That seems most likely. They never asked me to go with them.

She was a heavy one, that mother. Ratatouille and I would sweat like beggars trying to maneuver her as she sat on a simple wooden chair holding on for dear life and grunting like a pig—her nylon stockings rolled dismally about her ninety-pound ankles, the flab from her underarms resembling the ears of large elephants, her long white hair uncombed, her skin pockmarked and acne ridden, her breath foul and her face unwashed—down into a sunlight that had no use for her.

Her name, by some force of Fate or coincidence or just plain dumb luck, was also Irma, and she wrote poetry for Catholic magazines.

Often on my way to work, whenever I had work that is, I would start down the stairs only to hear my name grunted through a partly opened door. "Mr. Raymond," she would say, "My Bernie has left me for the day. Would you mind terribly mailing my letters for me?" I would hold my nose, step quickly into the room, take the sweaty postcards from her meaty hand, and then back out, saying, "No problem. No problem at all."

On the way to the mailbox, I would turn the postcards over and read them. The cards contained religious verses, handwritten in dark blue ink:

> *Dear God, Thank You for this Earth,*
> *For the horizon and its cloudless rim.*
> *Thank you for Christ's rebirth.*
> *Tonight, Tonight I pray to Him.*

or

> *Sweet Mary, how your eyes hurt.*
> *Sweet Mary, are you in pain like me?*
> *Sweet Sweet, Mary, all this shall end,*
> *And I too shall be like thee.*

On any given week, there would be hundreds of those poems going out in all directions.

I once asked Ratatouille what magazines would publish such stuff.

"Church magazines," he told me. "Church magazines."

I suppose I should have turned the cards over and checked out the exact names and addresses, but I was more fascinated by the poems. I hadn't attended community college for nothing. "What do you think of them?" Ratatouille once asked me. We were standing in front of our rundown building watching the cerebral palsy victims being loaded onto small yellow buses. They were heavy in their wheelchairs and did not float. How could God be so miserable to His own creations must have been a question that frequently crossed both of our minds as we contemplated pain made manifest in so much distorted and limping and drooling and uncoordinated flesh. The card he held out to me began, "I am God's Messenger! I help spread the good news." If I ever received any good news, I certainly would help spread it.

"I don't know," I answered. "I'm not a poet. Maybe there are people who like that sort of thing."

"It's garbage," Ratatouille said, tossing his stack of cards onto the street where pigeons and rats and dogs and weather could befoul them. I never did that. No matter what I thought of the verses, I always mailed them. What harm could it do? And maybe God would read them, change his mind about the sick, lame, and halt.

Maybe He would be so moved by the fat lady's devotion, He would heal everyone, including Ratatouille's dead brother. Or do you go to heaven with all your wounds healed? Or all the sores running? What about Christ's hands? You'd think they would be healed by now.

"All she does all day," he said, offering me a cigarette, Pall Malls, a brand I did not smoke and he knew it, "is sit in her chair writing garbage."

"As long as it makes her happy," I said, trying to be helpful.

"I doubt it. How can she be happy if she ever looks out her window and sees the cripples across the street? How can God get away with that shit?"

You could take a gun and shoot her, I suppose, I thought. I did not say it, though, for fear he would go ahead with it. A man who shoots people to cure toothaches is capable of any atrocity. Just like our Creator, who also destroys people to cure headaches. If he had any love left for his mother, he certainly did not show it. But he rarely missed a meal with her, and he kept her as well fed as he could. I guess that is showing love, now that I think of it.

But he was a mystery, all right.

Once I was walking through a large clothing store with my former boss, a man who used to own a bar where I would perform close-up tricks. There was a barbecue pit in the store and I had gathered together all kinds of steaks to be barbecued. Mammoth steaks. Sea Lion steaks. Lion steaks. I put the steaks on the barbecue, and then my ex-boss and I started down the stairs. Soon we were all the way across town. We were in another store, and there was a green carpet. I floated lightly over the top of it. I was in mid-air and floating.

But my ex-boss, weighed down by all manner of business concerns, could not float. Only I could. My only concern was that barbecue in his other store. I knew the steaks were burning and there was going to be a big fire and, even if I could float, I couldn't get back to them in time. We spoke in parables.

Maybe later, after Bernard had gone inside, I would rescue his mother's handiwork from the gutter and drop them into the mailbox. Maybe. As we grow older it becomes more difficult to know what course of action to take. Too many variables. Too many good deeds coming to nothing.

"Do you know how to float a woman?" Ratatouille asked me.

"Yeah, I know how to float a lady. I've never done it though. I never could afford the equipment."

"Suppose I bought you the equipment, could you do it?"

"Yeah. Sure. If you bought the equipment, *you* could do it."

"I don't want to do it," he said, staring at two high school girls crossing the street. "I want a professional magician to do it. It's got to be done right."

I couldn't figure him out, and standing on the street, across from all the cerebral palsy victims, was making me uncomfortable. Perhaps it was the sun. The sun was giving us all a beating. "You want a private show?" I asked. "Is that what it is?" I would enjoy levitating high school girls. I ask you, is it true that dreams of floating have some reference to orgasm? But then show me something in life that doesn't have reference to orgasm. Maybe the postcards from Ratatouille's mother.

"Not quite." He watched the girls walking away from him, their pretty rear-ends, their long red hair. I knew that Ratatouille had been married. Once. He came home one day and found a set of index cards kept by his wife. On the index cards were notes about her boyfriends: *Jack—He'll do if there is nobody else around. John—A good lover. Milton—Reminds me too much of my husband.*

Ratatouille took one look through the cards and moved out. Went back home to Mother. If I could feel sorry for him, I would have, but, in truth, the more I thought about the story, the more I laughed at it. What kind of a woman would be so organized? What kind of orgasms would she have? What kind of a man would marry such a woman? Of course, she wanted her husband to know she was fooling around. But then I'm not a psychiatrist. I only float things. Just as I am trying to float this story past you.

"Look," he said at last, "you want to make some money?"

"Sure. Who doesn't?"

"Sure. Who doesn't? If I tell you something, will you laugh?"

"Try me."

"I have a client," he said, as if he were lawyer, "who wants to make love to a woman while she floats in mid-air." He didn't look at me. He stared across the street at the line of yellow buses with their electronic chairlifts. A gray-haired woman was leading a child by the hand. His feet were turned inward. The child walked awkwardly upon his toes. His head flopped uneasily from side to side. Bernard waited for the words to sink in. If I had been younger and more innocent, perhaps I would have been shocked, but, in truth, the idea had occurred to myself from time to time. I just never had the opportunity or the courage or even the right woman.

"That sounds good to me," I said.

Was it a sigh? Bernard seemed relieved that I did not find the idea repugnant. Indeed it would be difficult for me to find an idea that would be as repugnant as Bernard himself. Why did I spend so much time talking to him? What was I waiting for? What did I want from him?

"All right. You get the equipment, send me the bill. Learn to float a lady and there's an extra two grand in it for you. Plus, you get to keep the equipment."

"That's generous enough," I said. "But what about the woman to be levitated? Does your client have a special woman in mind? If so, the plan might not work. I mean, it does take some practice on the part of the one to be levitated."

"We'll supply the woman. Her name is Irma. My client doesn't want to know how it's done. Just do it."

The yellow buses across the street were pulling away from the curb. The hallway of the building was jammed with wheelchairs. What kind of mad god could ever levitate them?

"You want to tell me anything about the client?" I asked.

"No"

"I didn't think so."

"Tell us when you're ready. We'll hire a hotel room. My client will come to the room where you will levitate his mistress in mid-air, and then he will make love to her."

"Do I watch?"

He shrugged. "Enjoy yourself. And find a place for me to hide where I can look on too."

"Does he know the floating that lady is a trick."

"He doesn't want it to be a trick."

"Nobody wants floating to be a trick. Nobody wants God to be a trick, either. But that's the way things are. It's not like the movies, you know. He'll be close to her, on top of her, so to speak. . . ."

Bernard smiled. "So to speak. . . ."

"He'll see how it's done."

"Fool him. He's got a lot of money. Enough money to buy a First Folio if he wants to. Do it well, and we all come out ahead."

"How does Irma feel about all this?"

"I don't know. You'll have to ask her, I guess."

And then we went inside. I don't know what became of the postcards tossed into the street. Perhaps the wind lifted them into thin air, carried them to a distant city where every broken reader of inspirational verse became enchanted.

On the morning of Irma's debut performance with Sammy Lau, I awoke with a burning sensation throughout my body. With love, my brain hummed. The scheme was mad. I knew I couldn't go through with it. Mad. Mad from start to finish. I made up my mind to skip town and take the floating gear with me. Rummaging through my belongings, I found an unused postcard showing a couple of palm trees on a beach I would never step unbroken foot upon. I hastily wrote:

Sweet Irma, how your eyes hurt me.
Sweet Irma, are you in pain like me?

Of course, I was going to be in remarkable pain once Sammy and Bernie noticed my unremarkable absence. As I hit the sidewalk with my cardboard suitcases, I wondered what had become of the postcards Bernie had tossed onto the street, into the gutter. Perhaps the wind had lifted them into thin air, carried them to a distant city where every broken reader of inspirational verse became enchanted, where nothing was anchored, tied down, where every single thing was

floating . . .

Notes from the
Committee of Grief

⌒

Hynes, telling a ribald story about a blind woman and the Pope, was at one end of the room and I was at the other. The joke, of course, was in poor taste, especially on Committee Meeting Day, but that's the way Hynes was. That's the way we all were, but it might have been good to keep our more bawdy sides in check, especially in light of the disasters pouring in left and right:

Athens, Greece. A heat wave, in which temperatures soared over 100 degrees for six straight days, has been listed as the cause of at least 260 deaths. A spokesperson at the First Aid Center in Athens said that 260 persons had died in hospitals from heat-related problems.

Trying to keep my ears and mind off Hynes' hyenaic brayings, I stood with my hands behind my back. I kept my gaze fastened to a blind accordion player on Wicklow Street. Heat-related problems, I thought. Isn't that we all have been suffering for lo these many decades, especially in light of the Greenhouse Effect and Temperature Inversions. Do I turn around to face my colleagues? How can I keep my mind on anything with Hynes' slobbering jokes across the Committee Room.

"Spare me!" I told Hynes. "I am in no mood to be trifled with."

He removed his finger from his light brown moustache. I had offended him. "You're never in a mood to be trifled with, Croften. Never. Never. Never."

"That's a lot of nevers," I told him, as we took our seats. Ms. Tam, 27, the youngest member of the Committee on Grief, filed in. We were mostly a subset of the Disaster and Crisis Bureau, and many of us, myself and Hynes included, had been on the Committee for nearly two decades. It was our job to frame letters of sympathy to victims. Not the kind of job one would take if one were looking for a lot of laughs.

Not the kind of job one would take if one could get any other kind of work whatsoever. Progress is an optical illusion, opiate of the high masses. Hynes completed his story and there was laughter all around. I didn't laugh. I refused to give into the absurdity of the situation. Four grown men and four grown women trying to provide machine gun bursts of comfort while all along thinking: Pajama party. I looked at my brown shoes and whistled. My shoes, as usual, needed polishing.

"Don't mind Crofton," Hynes announced. "You know he doesn't approve of levity in any form."

Maria Tierney, aged 40, was the coordinator of the meetings. She had thick blonde hair and wore a silver peek-a-boo suit. When I first started on the Committee I had thoughts of dating her, but she quickly put my hopes to rest. Administered Extreme Unction to my libido.

Marie, the quintessential traffic cop, held up her right hand and smiled.

"That will be enough of that!"

Yes, I thought, that will be enough of that. Unfortunately there is never never never enough of that. More nevers than we ever need. O'Connor was at my right. He was still wearing his ten-year-old black overcoat. He was always in mourning. He should have been a priest instead of a Victim Organizer—a fifty- year-old white-haired small-time politico chomping upon his unlit cigar and shuffling papers at a rate approaching the speed of light. "What does the day hold?" he asked in all earnestness.

What does the day hold? That phrase suited O'Connor to a T. It was the depth of his curiosity. Lately, I have only been interested in age. Outside on Wicklow Street, in stifling heat, the accordion player tapped out another stanza of "Terrorism, Tourists and Moi." A favorite of mine.

"Let's see," Marie said, trying to take O'Connor seriously, trying to take us all seriously. "There's a fire on a Sergek coastal vessel at Sarnchonpo. 71 killed."

Now it was Hynes' turn to whistle. "71?"

"So far," O'Connor added, doodling on his black-lined paper.

Marie paid us no heed. She rushed on, as she did at every other Committee meeting. So much to get through. "Seven truckloads of government dynamite explode in Cali, Colombia. An estimated 1,000 killed."

"A thousand killed means at least 5,000 letters," O'Connor said. He removed his soggy cigar and set it down upon the white table-cloth. Ah, what a stain was there!

"Just run them through the computer," Julia Parnell suggested. She was thirty-two, as plain as the nose on her face, and a direct descendant of the Irish Martyr. She never let anybody forget it. As if anyone would want to.

"More anonymous empathy from the Empathy Board," Hynes snorted with disgust.

"Earthquake in Leninakan." Maria proffered an 8 x 10 glossy of a man holding a dead three-year-old girl in his arms. I took it. "That man there is Diaz Pelletreau. Address on the back."

I turned the photo over. Local, I noted. "I'll take this one." Every once in a while it is good to volunteer for a Grief Assignment (GA's, as they are known) because it keeps our superiors happy. For what does it say over every doorway in the Sympathy Sector? KEEP ONE'S SUPERIORS HAPPY.

Not quite Dantean, but close enough. Abandon All Hype Ye Who Enter Here.

"Floods in southeast Darban leave 100,000 homeless. Explosion in a coal mine near Springhill, Nova Scotia, kills 76 miners, others trapped. Fire in the Montrose Helioport. 208 firefighters injured." Maria's voice was taking on its glazed quality. So much to get through. "Marover Corps transport plane crashed near Charles, February 14. 40 Marovers killed. The entire crew lost."

"I'll take that one," O'Connor said. I sighed. It was clear that O'Connor was bucking for a promotion. Hynes' right hand was resting heavily on Ms. Parnell's upper thigh. I couldn't see it, but I could sense it. A nose for news as the say. And nudes. Though my sex life had been dead for years.

Maria continued: "April 3rd. Thirteen persons were killed and nearly 600 injured when a passenger train plunged into the 'Canyon of Death,' in the Coluna Province of Mexico."

"Canyon of Death?" Hynes asked, rubbing his finger over his moustache. His right hand remained where it was. "Who makes up those things?"

"The Nomenclature Bureau," Ms. Parnell said, her voice barely a whisper.

"Who would buy a ticket to ride a train to the Canyon of Death. Doesn't that seem to be just asking for trouble?"

The committee members laughed. I merely shook my head and placed the photo of Diaz Pelletreau into a manila folder. In my head, I started to compose my letter to him. I could use Fax Form #2871 if I chose to, but sometimes I feel the need to come up with a fresh phrase. Otherwise one's work becomes too much of a grind. Old Testament's Job in another context.

"A bus fell over a precipice near the St. Bernard Monastery in Switzerland. Seventeen persons were killed."

Maria held out Form #48096.

Ms. Parnell took it. She was the expert on bus crashes. Hynes loved the trainwrecks. O'Connor usually handled explosions. The other members of the Committee—Henchy, Tam, and Shultz—

kept reaching for the forms until the steel table resembled a blizzard of sorrow. Maria didn't miss a beat: "There were 654 deaths over Independence Day weekend. Here's the list." Shultz coughed, took the form, buried it in a folder. She was an Aberdeenan Scot with a touch of tuberculosis. She needed to get in as much overtime as possible. Overtime. A euphemism for Eternity.

"There were 873 monorail fatalities over the New Year's Holiday."

Henchy was over six-foot-seven, a former basketball star. He was in his late forties, and his prose was going to seed, not that it was ever very stirring. Our Committee, however, felt it was important to recruit celebrities. It brightened the day of the mourners to receive a note with the autograph of a well-known person at the bottom. If push came to shove, the mourners could auction off the signature and buy an aphrodisiac. Scotch. Or a coffin. Unfortunately most of us, Henchy included, had taken to using the automatic signature machines. There are only so many letters a person can sign in a single day.

"A woman and her husband fell to their deaths when the bridge over the River Milpaso collapsed."

Outside the Committee Room, the accordion player, in spite of the heat, persisted.

2

The meeting broke up after 6:00 P.M. The final item on Ms. Tierney's agenda concerned a fallen power line. Some 42 persons and an elephant electrocuted. Fried spit. Tam, the white-haired writer of obscene limericks (redundant?), grabbed it for his group. Then Hynes told a story about a man and a dog. Quite Chekhovian, and not at all like Hynes. Afterwards, he and Ms. Parnell fondled off together, probably to some short stay hotel. Not wanting to pass any moral judgments upon my co-workers, I wished them well: "Toodaloo." And Hynes a married man. I packed my briefcase and watched them go. Watched everybody go. Henchy, Tam, and Schultz—a trio whose names reminded one of solicitors' officers, not solicitous, of course—adjourned to a narrow Pub called Indon, where the candles burned with luxury and the ale tasted of civilized colonies far off to the East.

Not having anything better to do but to go over the Abstracts of the Proceedings and to fax them to my Superiors (How was it possible at my age that I should have so many superiors? A failing of character my mother might have said. "What mother with a shape upon her lap," etc.), I returned to my office to compose the compulsory Letter of Condolence to what was his name? Diaz Pelletreau. How gracious to work for a people whose sole concern is the welfare of one another, to weep copious tears at the tax-payers' expense. Before, money had been flung to the winds for laser bombers and Venutian rocketships; now funds were flowing into our Committee by the truckload. Where was all that money going? I wondered. Not into my salary. I could barely support the sleeping quarters assigned to a person of my rank and station. I had a space off Igapo. It was filled to overflowing with absence. Even when I was there, I wasn't there.

I sat down at my computer terminal and started to work my way through the files:

Dear Mr. _____ (I left the name blank so that I could check the spelling of the name of God's suffering servant):

I cannot tell you how much I share your sorrow for the loss of your daughter. I know that there is nothing I can say at this time to relieve you of your grief. Nor should I desire to do so, for at times such as these it is right to grieve. I am certain that your daughter was the entire world to you and now you are standing in a world without a world. But it is not a world without meaning. The meaning evolves from the knowledge that you are not alone. There are many like myself who reach out to you, saying the same foolish words over and over again, the words of comfort that are no comfort, the prayers at a time when you think there is no one to pray to.

It says in the Book of Proverbs: "All the days of the afflicted are evil," but he that is of a merry heart hath a continual feast. I have never understood how one can have a merry heart in this world. I am certain your heart is not merry. Nor is mine.

I shall not attempt to make sense of the disaster that has befallen you. It makes no sense. But you must not add to the sorrow shared by your relatives and friends by doing harm to yourself. It is heroic to continue. Your daughter is still with you. Forever for always. If I could say anything to bring her back to life, I would. We all would. But think of all our lives embodying her life, bringing her back to life by performing millions of small, trivial tasks.

Should you wish to reach me any time of the day or the night, do not hesistate to call. I am in Section 9 of the Sympathy Sector. Extension 440.

Yours,
Crofton Milius Rosk

I reread the document, not at all pleased at how closely it followed Fax Form #2871. But there really is only so much a man can do. A thankless task at best. I typed in the correct name, double-checking, for once in Sector 5 a series of letters was misaddressed and we never heard the end of it. A national scandal that evolved into a vote of no confidence for the Trioptic Party. I typed in Mr. Pelletreau's address, pressed the transmission button, and off it went.

A good day's work, I thought. A good day's work. I was so exhausted, I fell asleep in my chair, imagining Hynes and Parnell in exotic postures of love. Or erotic postures of lust. Or whatever posturings they preferred.

3

April 26. San Andres de Bocay. A Brazilian airliner carrying 111 persons crash-landed during a blinding rainstorm. The jet skidded on the runway and crashed into a wall. All 111 persons on board were reported killed.

What does the day hold?

4

A predawn fire. Four days after the Committee Meeting, I had arisen at 6:00 A.M. to watch the soft pink sky through the pillars and towers of Sector 9. I couldn't sleep because the night before I had received a phone call from a man calling himself Diaz Pelletreau. At first, I could not place the name, but he identified himself as one of the survivors of the earthquake. After a few moments everything fell into place. He was being transported to Sector 11, and he wondered if I might meet with him.

"Of course," I said. "If there's anything I can do to help you, you know I shall. Where shall we meet?"

The voice (was it Pakastani? Hindi?) faltered. It was soft and musical, but seemed much further away than Sector 11. When I tried the monitor, the screen remained a perfect blank, which was the way it often is when the person placing the call wishes not to be seen.

"Anywhere you wish," he said. "I am new here. Perhaps you can suggest a place?"

"Yes, Yes, Yes," I said, my head churning. I turned over a few matchbook covers I kept in a plastic dish. "I understand. How about the Indon. It's a well-established Pub at G9/Sector 10."

"Indon?"

I spelled it for him. Still, no image on the monitor. A monitor without an image is a person without a heart.

"I'll be there."

"You won't have any trouble finding it."

"I'll be there."

"Shall we say 1800 hours?"

"I shall be there. How shall I recognize you?"

"I have a picture of you. Let me find you." What had I done with the photo given to me at the meeting? To say the least, my files were, like my shoes, unpolished.

"You carry a briefcase?"

"For you I'll carry a briefcase," I told him, though I wasn't quite certain why I had phrased it that way. "Look for the Insignia of The Disaster and Crisis Bureau."

"Bye," he said.

"Bye."

That was all, I thought? Bye? The heart of the monitor, blank as it was, went black. For some reason I thought of my mother who had died two years before. I had not felt enough grief. Could never feel enough grief for someone who had spent so much time in one's life, for someone who held such presence. More presence in absence, they say. The ultimate paradox.

5

What does the day hold?

The question came straight from the camel's mouth as it were, from O'Connor's own beefy lips. Late for my meeting with Mr. ___ (in truth I could never remember his name), I had entered the elevator of my Habitat to see O'Connor in his black coat, his perpetual calendar of despair, waiting for me or for someone to pounce upon. He was carrying a bouquet of semi-wilted purple flowers. Irises? I wouldn't know. The last time I had fresh flowers in my sleeping quarters was when I attempted to seduce Ms. Tierney, but she turned out to be allergic. To the flowers *and* to me. Sneezing was as close to orgasm as she got all evening.

"A fire in Sector 12," he announced the moment he saw me. "A candle affixed to a wall tipped over and ignited a sofa. Entire family of four burned to death."

"Really." I said, my eyes glazing over.

"Your staff want to handle it?"

I shook my head. Someone was putting an axe inside of my brain. Where is Lizzie Borden when you need her?

"Shultz is in the hospital again. You want to come with me? These flowers are for her."

Jesus, I thought. Doesn't he ever give up? "No. Thanks for the invitation, but I have an appointment."

"Where?"

Where? My, you're a blunt man, I thought. The elevator had brought us to the lobby, and, because he was a comrade in the battalion of tears, I told him. I spilled out the details of the phone call. O'Connor was a willing listener. You should have thought I was reciting *Terrorism Tourism and Moi* to him.

After I concluded, under the watchful eyes of Habitat Security, O'Connor shook his head. "You know something, Croften?"

"What?"

"I've been a member of our sub-committee for nearly as long as you have, and in all those years, not once has anyone I have ever written to called me up to request a meeting."

"Strange, isn't it?"

"Of course," he said, "I have gotten notes and letters thanking me for my concern."

"Of course."

"Thanking me for my sympathies. But never a call. Never a face-to-face meeting."

"It is highly irregular."

I started to break away, but as I headed through the glass doors, O'Connor called after me.

"Wait! Maybe I had better go with you," he said, taking my elbow. I would rather hang by my thumbs.

"Just in case," he added.

"Just in case of what?"

"In case he turns out to be a fanatic or something."

A fanatic about grief and grieving. That's a new one I thought.

"No, thanks," I told him, politely extricating myself from his grip. "I'll go ahead, and maybe I'll meet you and Shultz at the hospital," I lied.

O'Connor stepped backward. I saw his reflection in the double doors. He was crestfallen. I had mortally offended him. Offending people, that's my middle name.

"I'll tell you all about it," I promised, and made my escape into a hothouse of carbon emissions, leaving O'Connor to contemplate 32 prisoners in the Fortaglia Detention Camp who died after inhaling toxic fumes from polyurethic padding in the jail cells. The world of Justice is so old-fashioned, I thought.

6

He was there, all right. Just the way he said he would be. Mr. Diaz Pelletreau. Seated in a secluded corner of the narrow, candlelit pub.

He was facing front, scanning everyone who entered. He recognized me because of the insignia on the briefcase. He called my name: "Mr. Rosk."

"Mr. Pelletreau?" I had written his name on a slip of paper. I was glad that he had recognized me, for I do not think I would have recognized him.

He was greatly changed from the man in the photo. His hair was close-cropped, his narrow face trimmed with wire spectacles, a slight man, couldn't have weighed more than 130 pounds, wearing striped pajamas or a pajama-like suit. His skin was dark, swarthy.

He didn't stand up, though I thought he might. It is the usual thing to do. He merely nodded his head while I slid into the booth beside him. I placed my briefcase upon the table, undid the snaps in order to pull out any documents he might require. So many persons, caught up in their immediate emotions, forget the required paperwork.

"Have anything you want," I told him. "The Committee is footing the bill."

"Just coffee," he said.

"Have something more," I told him. "The Indon has a rather good menu for a Pub, that is if you like Pub food.

"I've eaten," he said. There was a flatness to his voice. He removed his spectacles and wiped his eyes with his shirt sleeve. "Coffee is fine."

"Two coffees," I told the waiter. The waiter was not pleased, but that was his problem.

Mr. Pelletreau pushed a four-page pamphlet across the top of my briefcase.

"What's this?" I asked.

He shrugged. "Something someone gave me on the way in."

"GIVE PHILOSOPHY A CHANCE TODAY. Commit thy way unto Higher Mathematics," the cover page read. "FIRST CONDITION: To Repent of your sins write them down—accept the Laws of Calculus as your personal Saviour from Sin. We must live our lives the way Newton and Liebnitz taught us to live them."

I had seen such pamphlets before. Many times. "Except that a person know Mathematics he cannot see the Kingdom of Wisdom."

A few days before, as I was emerging from an exhibition on The New Urban Landscape, a young lady is a saffron robe had handed me such a pamphlet. With so much tragedy on the horizon, it was inevitable that new cults would spring up.

I turned the pamphlet over, opened my briefcase, and slipped it inside.

"You didn't bring me all the way into Sector 10 to discuss salvation with me, did you?"

The waiter, in spite of our paucity of food and drink orders, was quite prompt with the coffees.

"No," Mr. Pelletreau said. "I've come a long way to discuss this." He reached down to the bench we were sitting upon and brought forth a folded piece of paper. As soon as he started to unfold it, I recognized exactly what it was—a printout of my letter from the Sympathy Sector. He spread it on the table and wiped his hand over it several times, pressing the wrinkles out of it.

"Why?"

The question took me aback. "What do you mean why? You *know* why. We thought you needed to hear from somebody."

"Not from you!"

"Grief is not easy to bear alone," I told him. "We do the best we can."

"Not from you," he repeated, this time with such intensity that several patrons of the Pub turned their heads. "You had no right to write me. No right at all. None." He grabbed the letter and flung it toward my face.

"What are you talking about? It's my job!" I told him.

"You bastard!" he cried. "You take it upon yourself to write me a letter when you don't even know me! When you don't even care if I exist or not."

He was losing control, standing up and shouting. "What am I to you? Nothing? Less than nothing! And you intrude upon my grief?"

"Of course we care. Why don't you think we don't care? I took the time to write you, didn't I? It could happen to any of us!" I shouted back at him.

I wasn't about to be intimidated.

"I spit upon your letter. I spit upon you." Two burly waiters started toward us. My friend let loose with steady streams of saliva, first upon the letter and then upon me. I put my arm in front of my face.

"Stop it!" I cried. "You don't know what you're doing."

"Don't you ever write to me again. Ever. You have no right. *You have no right*." He picked up the white mug and hurled the coffee into my face. The waiters were upon him, but it was too late. I was screaming. It hurt like hell. "You never even met my daughter. You had no idea what she was like!"

"My eyes!" I cried.

The words were spilling out of him in torrents. "An angel she was. An angel. And she was mine! You can't take her away from me with your filthy letter."

"My eyes!" I blindly lunged for my attacker while one of the waiters frantically dabbed my face with a towel.

"Keep calm, Mr. Rosk," one of the regulars said. "You'll be all right."

"I want that bastard out of here! Out of here!"

"The next time you write me a letter like that, I'll kill you," my attacker called to me. "I'll kill you. Then someone can write your parents a letter."

I managed to open my eyes in time to see my attacker being dragged across the floor of the candlelight room. Members of the Indon staff were all over him. After all, I was known in the place, and he was not. Whose side were they going to take?

"Ice," one of the older waiters said. "Ice is the best thing to put upon a burn." He turned to a companion. "Get Mr. Rosk some ice."

"I'll be all right," I said. "It doesn't burn that much." I pushed the helpful hands away. I was more startled than burned. More hurt than burned. I sank to the bench and tried to catch my breath, tried to sort out what was happening. Was the whole world insane?

"Shall I call the police?" my waiter friend asked.

I shook my head. "I'll be all right. Just leave me alone," I told him." I felt everyone was staring at me.

"Let me bring you something to drink." Another waiter returned with a bucket of ice and some clean towels.

"Just leave me alone," I told them, perhaps with a bit more vehemence than was called for. "Leave me alone!"

"Very well, Mr. Rosk. But if you need anything, anything at all, just let us know." He tapped his friend upon the arm and they returned to the bar. It wasn't that fights were unknown in pubs, but they certainly weren't common in the Indon.

I sat at my table for about twenty minutes, trying to regain my composure. The last thing I did before I finally worked up courage to leave was to find my crumbled letter. I retrieved it from the floor, placed the document in my briefcase and snapped the case shut. The letter did belong to me. The Law would uphold me upon that point. Should it ever come to Law.

Two weeks later, when our Committee was scheduled to assemble, the meeting was cancelled because of the death of Ms. Shultz. We were, of course, saddened by the announcement, and right away our minds were set racing about who was going to replace her. Another celebrity might be in order.

I was supposed to go to the Memorial Service, but, in truth, I was quite far behind in my work, and I had quite a few notes to go over for my superiors.

February 16. Moscow. Fire broke out during rush hour at the Aviamotornaya Subway Station. At least 102 persons severely injured. 15 persons died when the moving surface of the escalator gave way and they were hurled into the mechanism.

Early March. Algiers. At least 300 spectators who had illegally climbed to the roof of the August 20 Stadium to watch a soccer match died when the roof collapsed.

March 12. Fires started by teams of arsonists destroyed whole tenement buildings near the Fotaglia Detention Camp . . . .

Really there was just too much to do. Really.

A Brief Account of Termites
Found in Africa (1871)

⌒

The man and the woman were seated in one of the back booths of the Dory Pub. And dimly lit it was, so that everyone seemed to resemble everyone else. One had to look closely at the sacs.

She was a woman in her mid-forties or so. A biologist whose husband, who had lost his left hand in Viet Nam, worked as a counselor in a private school in Manhattan. Teenagers were threatening suicide all the time, she reported Kroll as saying, difficult to understand them. They seem to have everything to live for. They had wealth. They had good educations. Their parents could open doors for them. But they were hell-bent upon destroying themselves. In journals they handed in to their teachers, they frequently alluded to suicide. Open windows frequently beckoned. Or crack. Nothing very tidy. The bodies were frequently placed upon display in pubs and bars and subway stations. Corpses to be a warning to the young.

And so many of the girls suffered from eating disorders. A diet of honey-ants, for example. Cravings for *Mystrium rogein.* They would devour handfuls and then throw them up.

But most of all—the girls had youth. Youth!

Ah, youth, Benjamin thought.

The man whose close-cropped head bobbed and nodded in the candlelight was nearing fifty, a college teacher himself, and was sitting with Renee at a bar for a few drinks before they both took off to their separate obligations. The night before Benjamin had taken his four-year-old sons to a high school dance concert at the school where his wife Samantha, whom everyone called Sammy, taught Music with a capital M (Renee herself was studying the Harpsichord; it was her refuge from the constant paper-grading and commuting and family disputes), and there were all those deliciously nubile bodies parading before him in leotards and tights and their ripe breasts and their clean faces and most of all youth. Youth! How could he possibly concentrate upon the music, upon the movement, when it was the movement of his entire life being choreographed before his eyes. To be a teenager once again, instead of being locked into a life without possibilities, whose every movement was circumscribed, programmed. The young women at the bar were so young.

"What are you doing this summer?" Benjamin asked, as the waiter brought a second round of dark ale. He himself felt 800,000,000 years old.

"You won't believe it," Renee said, sitting back in the dim light of the pub booth. She raised her arms to adjust her brown hair, took the rubber band from her teeth and snapped it over her hair. Her face was thin. Her eyes tired. She had been working too hard and her mother was ill, another round of operations to be faced.

"Try me. I believe anything," Benjamin confessed, testing his drink, testing his own capacity for alcohol. Counting the second drink with Renee, he was now working on his seventh mug of the afternoon. It was more difficult than ever to come up with reasons to remain sober. For example, he thought, he didn't have to drive. It was only a mere eight blocks from the bar to home, from semidarkness with free *hors d'oeuvre* into a well-lit domicile where everything had to be paid for, including the light, the garbage, the electricity, the heat, the towels, the laundry, the insects: *"Whenever they pass all the rest of the animal world is thrown into a state of alarm."*

"Botswana," she said.

"Botswana? I'm uncertain where the hell that is."

"Africa," she said.

"Oh, hell. I knew that," he said. "Give me some credit for knowing something. *They stream along the ground and climb to the summit of the lower trees, searching every leaf to its apex . . . .*" In his exuberance he splashed the black wood of the table with ale.

"Sorry."

"Sorry," she replied.

"Sorry." He motioned for the waiter.

"Are you still working on Bates?"

"I've given up on that," he said. "I've given up on everything."

"You shouldn't," she said.

"It's not as if Master Bates hasn't been written about before."

"It's all to do again."

"Over and over and over. . . . So what's in Botswana? Shrunken heads?"

"A friend whom I've. . . ."

"Ah yes. A friend. Excuse me." He stood up and stumbled toward the bathrooms. Queens and Kings. Knights and Damsels. Queens and Drones. Why don't they just put Men and Women like the old days. Why was it getting necessary to have a college education to go to the bathroom? He was pleased to see the urinals stocked with ice. It gave him a feeling of well-being to piss on ice . . . *booty is plentiful, they concentrate.*

And now to die with all the smaller species. They were all so young. O to live in his father's house again, with his mother and sisters, and to understand the multitude of generosities that had been his life. A man whom I survive to give love . . . heigh-ho. Piss on Henry Walter Bates.

Was Renee miffed because he had risen up mid-sentence? Or was it mid-sentence? Sentenced to live? One had to cultivate manners in order to survive what with everybody coming at you from all different directions at once. Young students to whom booty is beautiful. Yes. On booty they concentrate. He checked his fly: What's it like out? I don't know. I don't keep it out.

On the mirror over the sink, the tattered sign read:

THE HEAD
Of the Renowned Bandit
JOAQUIN
Will be EXHIBITED
For one day only August 17th
—at the Dory Pub

Plus The Hand of the Notorious Robber and Murderer Three-Fingered Jack. Joaquin and Three-Fingered Jack were captured by the state rangers under the command of Captain Harry Love at the Arroya Cantina on July 24th. No reasonable doubt can be entertained in regard to the identification of the head now on exhibition as being that of the notorious robber, Joaqin Murietta, for it is recognized by hundreds of persons who had seen him and described him in the splendid etchings that accompanies this happy announcement.

As further proof, the hand of Joaquin's evil accomplice, Three-Fingered Jack Garcia, has been removed from its more ordinary position and is preserved in a jar of alcohol for display at the public exhibition.

He read it twice, took note of the date, and returned to Renee. Harry Love. Harry Harry Love. "I couldn't hold it in any longer." He slid into the booth and signaled for the waitress. "A friend *who*?"

"A few years ago, Kroll and I rented an apartment in Paris, but we showed up early and the people who owned it were still there. But they were very friendly and invited us in and entertained us. A woman with a son in his early twenties. Brilliant. A historian. She's brilliant, too. A photographer. She's been all over Europe. One country to another. Brad was speaking Hungarian and French before he was four years old. Once, when they were leaving Hungary to go to Paris, Brad turned to his mother to ask if they were ever coming back. 'No,' she said. 'They were never coming back.' 'Good,' he said. 'Now I can forget Hungarian.'"

He looked into her eyes and nodded. Yes. The languages of extreme otherness. He was uncommonly proud of his near-photographic memory.

"And so as a consequence of his upbringing he never felt he had a real home. We all became very close friends, a friendship out of the ordinary, and so last year Brad came to New York to visit us. While he was here, he decided to find the house where his grandfather died. It was a small farmhouse on Long Island and his grandfather had been buried in the yard, but when Brad finally located the house, everything had been torn down to make way for a highway. The only thing Brad managed to salvage from the trip was a fence-post which he believed had marked his Grandfather's grave. He had no reason to believe it, no logical reason. It was merely a feeling that came over him.

"When he came back from Long Island, he realized that he couldn't carry the fence post with him back on the plane, and he asked us to keep it for him. So we've kept his grandfather's soul for him in our study waiting for Brad to return. Except now Brad has decided to accept a two-year position in Botswana."

"At least you'll have someone to stay with out there," Benjamin, child of sorrow, said. "That'll save you a lot of money."

"Some. But let me finish. A couple of weeks ago, my Kroll and I noticed that there were a lot of ants in the kitchen. Big black ants. Hundreds of them. We never had so many ants before. And we watched them as they paraded toward the water bowl we leave out for the cat. A procession of ants going for the water. And then they turned around and trooped back to the fence post."

"There was a nest of ants living in the fence post?" Benjamin asked.

Renee nodded.

"What are you going to do about them?"

"Nothing. My husband wants to kill them, but they're carrying the spirit of Brad's grandfather. I won't let him. As soon as he starts killing the ants, I go out the door. I'll leave him. He knows it."

Benjamin laughed. "The man's a saint."

Somebody at the bar asked, "Where's the hand of Three-Fingered Jack?"

"Not here yet," the bartender said. "August 17th."

"I could be dead by then."

"Me too." The bartender set a bottle of Bushmills on the bar.

In *Tarzan of the Apes*, Tarzan discovers a child's primer. Although the pictures fascinate him, he is most taken by the letters of the alphabet which he thinks of as bugs: "The strange little bugs which covered the pages where there were no pictures excited his wonder and deepest thought." But were the bugs ants? Termites? *Daceton Armigeru?*

"Two nights ago Kroll was working on his computer when the ants started across the keyboard. They were on their way to the water again. And he just sat there and watched them."

"The man's a saint," Benjamin repeated.

"Oh no. He got on the phone and called Brad in Botswana and cursed him up one end and down the other. 'Come back here you sonuvabitch and get your goddamn fence post out of our apartment before we're swallowed alive by ants!'"

Now Renee was laughing.

The *Anomma* queen can lay 60,000 eggs in three days," Benjamin said, feeling a splendid warmth rising within his spirit. "Some colonies have more ants in them than the population of New York. Or Tokyo, I guess, which is the world's largest city. Or Mexico City. I can see the headlines now: 'Couple in Queens Devoured by 20,000,000 Ants. Nothing Left Except a Mysterious Fence Post and a Water Dish.'"

"I don't think it's going to come to that?"

"I think you should eat them," Benjamin said.

"Eat them?"

"Sure. Honey ants taste better than bee's honey."

"How do you know. Have you ever eaten them?"

He sat back in the dim light and patted his stomach. "Do I look like the sort of person who has missed out on any delicacy?" He felt embarrassed. He had to go to the bathroom again.

"Wasn't it Socrates who contended that the souls of philosophers would be reincarnated in the body of ants? How do you think Kroll and I would feel knowing we were eating the souls of philosophers."

"Hungry, I should think. I can't believe the souls of philosophers would provide enough nourishment to sustain a five-year-old child for two days. Anyway, be grateful they are not driver ants. My sister-in-law was with the Peace Corps in Kenya and every few months millions and millions of driver ants would march through the village, eating everything in sight. She and her roommate would sit on top of the kitchen table and watch them swarm through. One of the good things about it was that the ants ate all the other small pests. Did a remarkably good job of housecleaning."

"I don't know what kind of ants these are." Renee opened her pocketbook and pulled out a few crumbled bills.

"*Daceton Armigerum? Azteca Sericea?*" He was just kidding her. It was a small joy but a substantial one nevertheless. There were not many honorable ways a married man could touch a woman married to someone else. In his own briefcase there was a letter from an old friend, a letter written in red ink on pink paper, a letter terribly unhappy: "The person I'm doing my best to end a love relationship with had left a message on my machine that he was going to be out of town for several days—a week's vacation with his wife. O, twist the knife. Why did he even have to call—and at a time he knew I wouldn't be there to be a real person back. He didn't want a real person anyway."

"I don't know."

"Have fun in Botswana with Joachim," he said, trying to stand up to help her *with her fur coat.*

They tear their victims in pieces for easy carriage. . . . Yes, that is what termites do.

"Who's Joachim?"

"Sorry. I mean what's-his-name."

She shook her head. It didn't look like another head.

"I'll take care of the tip," he offered. Coins fell from his pockets onto the sawdust strewn floor.

"I have it." She counted out some coins and put on her coat. "This was nice, but I have to run. Kroll and I had a terrible argument last night about the ants. I have to get home to make certain he's still there."

She picked up her briefcase and pocketbook. Her papers and books weighed as much as she did. One needed the weight of objects to be kept from being blown away. One more copy of Henry Smeathman's 1871 edition of *Account of Termites Found in Africa.*

"Throw out the stupid fence pole."

"I can't."

They kissed, or at least brushed lips. The language of extreme otherness. And then he watched her go. The street was filled with strangers rushing home to other obligations.

"Swears he and his wife are sister and brother," the terrible letter read.

The Destruction of Iowa

$\sim$

In recent histories of our former colony, The United States of America, the destruction of Iowa has gone largely unnoticed, as well as it might in light of more recent and far-ranging cataclysms. As far as I have been able to ascertain, the story was buried in the back pages of the *New York Times* and the *Washington Post* and would have been forgotten completely had not my close friend, Wallace Sidey (pronounced with a long *I*) completed a dissertation on minor catastrophes of the late Twentieth Century. There is no doubt that many of the facts about the Iowa fiasco deserved to be made known to that small part of the general population that still reads. With Sidey's permission, the following account is placed before you in the hope that such a bizarre history will not repeat itself in our own enlightened republic.

It has been widely held that the opening salvo against the citizenry of Iowa was one arm of a revolutionary plot, a brilliant tactical stroke of black insurrectionists, This view cannot stand up under close examination. Mr. Sidey's research has laid that rumor to rest once and for all. Rather, on a sun-drenched afternoon in early summer, in a state that derived its name from a Sioux word that means "Sleepy Ones," the central computer for the Bell Telephone System in Iowa City suffered a micro-sleeping sickness of its own. In Dr. Sidey's reconstruction of the events, a program card emerged in a pile of outgoing bills, slipped through by mistake, and in less time than it takes to tell it, Mr. George Kruishank of nearby Windham received an incorrect phone bill.

It must be said in all fairness to the former inhabitants of the United States that one virtue which they possessed in great abundance, and which our own republic lacks, was a sense of humor. At the time of the Iowa Fiasco, there was hardly anyone in the United States who had not, at one time or other, suffered the indignity of a computer error. Most inhabitants, however, had learned, in the words of a noted comic strip of the time, to grin and bear it. Unfortunately, George Kruishank was an exception that goes to prove the rule: he lacked a sense of humor. In addition, his phone bill was for $13,267.84, and for the month he had been billed, he had been away on a hunting trip. Eyewitness accounts, coupled with photographs taken by the hunting party, substantiate the fact that G. K. had not used his own phone once during the month of June. Such are, or were, the ways of life.

As you might have suspected from the sparse description thus far given, George was quite pessimistic about the ethics of his fellow man, and that trait, in tandem with a lack of humor, made G. K. less than popular with his neighbors (Harris Street). If one were given to hyperbole (and cliché), one might freely state that the neighbors avoided the five-foot-nine hunter like the plague.

To return to this amusing anecdote, when George received the incorrect phone bill, he suspected that his next door neighbor, Willis Enright, had stolen into his house and had allowed his (Willis's) friends and relatives to make phone calls all over the globe and perhaps to places beyond the globe, leaving good old George to pick up the tab. Well, good old George was not going to pick up that tab. He checked the shells in his shotgun and shoved open his back door to find his next door neighbor sitting in the yard. Willis was a well-known practical joker and pulled some funny stunts before, but George had decided that this was one stunt Willis would not get away with.

"Howdy, George." Willis, sixty years old and bald, greeted his red-faced neighbor with a wan smile. He sat in a white wicker rocking chair, sipping lemonade and enjoying the sunset. This incident is largely substantiated by entries in Kruishank's five-year diaries, but I hope my readers will not be unduly upset if I take a few artistic liberties. Dr. Sidey agrees with me that the word *howdy* was a common greeting of the time and place. "Any bears chase you up a tree?"

George didn't laugh. He stopped, spread his legs wide apart, and cradled his shotgun in his arms. "I guess," he sputtered, "everybody was glad to see me go away, so they could get to my phone." By the time he reached the end of his sentence, his voice was nearly choking with rage. "Are you going to tell me what happened or not?"

Willis had often seen his next-door neighbor worked up over nothing, and so the latest outburst posed no real threat to him. "Get off your high horse, George, and set a spell," the retired banker replied calmly.

George pulled the phone bill from his trousers' pocket and tossed it into his neighbor's lap. "You see that? I got a phone bill for over thirteen thousand dollars, and I was away for the month. You see that?"

"I see it." Willis nodded his head sympathetically. He clucked his tongue.

"I wasn't even home, and I get a bill for over thirteen thousand dollars. I think somebody around here has been having fun at my expense, and when I find out who it is, I'm going to have a little fun of my own."

George studied his neighbor's face carefully, seeking some kind of clue, but Willis sipped his lemonade and displayed no sign of guilt. "Oh this? Yeah. I suspect a lot of people have been getting them. Some kind of mistake. If I were you, I'd call the phone company and get it straightened out right away."

"Yeah?"

"Yeah."

"All right, but I'm using your phone," George said, calming down slightly. "I'll be damned if I'm going to make any more calls on mine."

"It's all right with me." Willis jerked his thumb over his left shoulder. "You know where it is."

George took his shotgun with him, and without wiping his boots, he entered his neighbor's kitchen and dialed the phone company to complain about his bill. The ensuing conversations took almost an hour, and at the conclusion, the phone company insisted that no mistake had been made. G. K.'s bill was correct for the amount the phone was used.

Naturally.

George argued. He shouted. He complained. He threatened. His call was shunted from one supervisor to another. He received one small satisfaction. The head supervisor advised him to wait for his next bill, due at the end of August, and then simply to pay the corrected amount. The head supervisor was courteous throughout George's harangue. George finally gave up and went outside to have a lemonade with his neighbor.

In August the corrected bill arrived. The bill was $32.48 for July, and the still unpaid amount of $13,267.84 for June, making a total of $13,300.32. A printed slip expressed the hope that the bill would be paid promptly; otherwise phone service would be discontinued. As G. K. reread his bill for the fourth time, it dawned on him that he had been made a fool of. His neighbors had been using his phone illegally, and Willis had been stringing him along all that time, prompting George's hassles with the phone company. At five o'clock in the afternoon, Willis Enright was found dead with two shotgun wounds squarely in the chest.

The Enright murder is fully documented by local newspapers, as is the Kruishank trial. What was not documented and what has been brought to light by Sidey's research are Kruishank's activities from the time of his capture to the time of his trial. As revealed by notes in his diary, Kruishank quickly repented his hasty and irrational act against his neighbor. And meanwhile, the extreme publicity attending the murder had forced the phone company to reexamine G. K.'s phone bill. In September, G. K., released on $100,000 bail, received an adjusted bill for $82.50. The $13,000 error had been corrected. Alas, it was too much, too late. Willis Enright had been murdered, and G. K. had ruined his own life in the process. Night after sleepless night, Kruishank turned in his bed, vowing revenge on a society that had wronged him most grievously.

Five weeks before the swearing in of the jury, G. K. concocted a heinous scheme of retaliation. Knowing that money would be of very little use to him in the future, he withdrew his substantial life savings from the Windham National Bank, hired an expert who had worked on the phone company's computer, and began, in effect, his own billing operation. Drawing upon every resource opened to him, and making use of a small staff of secretaries, G. K. duplicated the phone company's bills down to their finest details, including the gray mailing envelopes with the return address. G. K.'s handpicked and highly paid staff turned to the Iowa City phone directory for a core mailing list, and by the first week in December, the United States mails carried thousands of incorrect bills to the innocent citizens of Iowa. Most of the phone bills were nominal, but some were for thousands of dollars. A few small bills were paid by G. K. himself just to get the computer humming.

And hum it did. As soon as unsuspecting subscribers began paying their bills and their miscoded computer cards entered the computer, the computer reacted wildly. It soon complicated matters, for it too began printing out incorrect statements for other customers. Mistake led to mistake, as it were, and soon numerous high-level executives began to go without sleep. All in all, December was not a joyous time for Iowa phone companies.

Within days, the phone company was besieged by letters of inquiry, swamped by poisoned pen notes, threatened with lawsuits, and inundated by representatives of numerous citizens' groups that had rapidly formed for consumer protection. Families who had innocently paid incorrect bills and who were hard-pressed for money for Christmas promptly pleaded for refunds. The phone company did not turn a deaf ear, but responded by mailing out a five-page, intricately detailed Request-for-Refund forms. As water solidifies to ice, so did the righteous indignation of the Iowans. A good number of prominent citizens, their sense of humor fading, refused to spend the time required to fill out the Request-for-Refund Forms, and many sent back the forms in shreds. Early in January, one high executive of the phone company stated that he thought the bills were not in error at all, and the entire commotion could be traced to a small number of black insurrectionists. Needless to say, that careless statement sent tempers soaring. One bright businessman had the foresight to begin marketing cotton pillows shaped like computers. These pillows were dubbed "Bellamies" by the local wags, in honor of Graham Bell, and it became a ritual of the festive season to burn one's Bellamy in effigy.

I wish it were possible for me to detail all the individual complaints sired by Kruishank's revenge, but since the space allotted to me is extremely limited, allow me to cite Harvey Miller and his family as a typical case.

Harvey Miller was the fifty-year-old owner of a trailer camp on the outskirts of Iowa City. When he received two widely differing phone bills in a single month and discovered that he had mailed the company eighteen dollars more than he should have, he called for a refund. The manager of the phone company was firm but polite. The bill had already been processed by the computer and had been stored. There was no recourse but to adhere to the company's rules, and thus Mr. Miller and his family received the five-page Request-for-Refund form. This was at a time of the year when the Income Tax people were also mailing out the thirty-page Federal Income Tax forms, but Harvey, Harvey's wife, and their ten-year-old son, Scotty, bent upon justice, spent the better part of three evenings checking old bills, locating the cancelled check, extricating the cancelled check from their bank before the regular monthly statement (a feat that required the filling out of two additional forms), and leaving no blank spaces on the refund form. As soon as the ink dried, the Request-for-Refund was placed into the mail. Six weeks later, they still had no reply.

Harvey Miller, his wife, his son, and his secretary each mailed letters of inquiry. Each received additional copies of the Request-for-Refund Form. The additional copies were ripped into shreds and flushed down the toilet. He immediately called the phone company. Unfortunately, he was only one of eighteen thousand other irate customers trying to reach the same branch, and so he could not get through. A recorded statement pleasantly informed him that "all agents were helping other customers," but if he would hold on, someone would answer as soon as possible. Miller held on for forty-five minutes before he slammed the receiver down. He tried three more times with no success. In a rage, he tore the phone off the wall.

Two days later Harvey Miller's grandmother got through, and the supervisor, a soft-voiced woman with a southern accent, assured her that a refund check had indeed been mailed four weeks previously. The supervisor assured the ninety-four-year-old woman that the company would have the post office trace the misplaced check.

Whether refund checks were actually mailed to the phone company's customers can be only a matter of conjecture. Dr. Sidey has found no evidence pro or con on the matter. However, if such checks were placed into the mail, it could not have happened at a more inopportune time, for the Postal System was still gasping under the intolerable burden of holiday mailings. Dr. Sidey has hypothesized that the phone company had slyly used the lost-mail tactic to divert anger away from its door and down the hall of governmental enterprise. Whether or not Dr. Sidey 's hypothesis is correct is beyond the scope of this paper. All I can do is point out that, indeed, in very short order, the Post Office was blamed for losing important checks. Warmed by rising tempers, the Aggrieved Citizens Committee of Iowa (ACCI) pressured the state legislature to investigate the phone company and the Post Office. Over fifty cases of physical assault upon mail carriers were recorded, and employees of the Post Office, rather than face increased hostility, voted to go on strike. The matter became further complicated when the Harveys, in accordance with 18,000 other citizens, stated in a written petition that they would pay no more phone bills until the refund checks were in hand. The phone company retaliated by discontinuing phone service. Over 12,350 phones were disconnected in Iowa City alone. A few days later, the central Post Office building in Iowa City was burnt to the ground. And bombs were set off in the phone company's offices. Sixteen employees were killed in the explosions. Families of the victims began to arm themselves. Handguns were being sold at the rate of six per minute throughout the state.

In view of their deepening troubles with the Post Office and with the electric companies, the citizens of Iowa began to doubt the accuracy of any bill. Perhaps Kruishank had mailed out rigged electric bills as well, but there is no evidence to substantiate that charge, and Dr. Sidey has found no mention of it in the five-year diary. However, it is a matter of record that over two-thirds of the persons involved in disputes with the phone company, not knowing where to draw the line, refused to pay their electric bills as well. Deprived of the mails, the electric company had set up numerous offices for the payment of bills, but few citizens took advantage of the convenience. To induce payment, the electric company began turning off electricity in a select number of neighborhoods, and soon high-level executives of the electric company were sucked into the whirlpool of hot-headed dispute. A group of patriots called the Minute Men publicly advocated a People's Revolution, and on January 11th, almost at the very hour when Kruishank's lawyer was making his closing remarks to the jury, generator plants in Windham and in West

Branch were sabotaged. Large portions of Johnson and Cedar counties were plunged into darkness. Wholesale looting started in the shopping centers, and so the Governor had no choice but to call up the National Guard.

The Governor appeared on television and read a public statement in which he appealed for citizens to control their tempers and to use common sense during these most trying hours. The Governor pledged that he would restore order as soon as possible and he hoped that he could lift martial law as soon as possible. The sale of handguns and small firearms continued unabated, and sporadic gunfire broke out in several parts of Iowa City, in Windham, and as far away as Springdale. In addition the postal workers were hopping mad about governmental interference in a local dispute about the safety of working conditions. The president of Local #3498 stated that unless the National Guard kept its hands off the mail, they would not be responsible for any violence that might occur. To strengthen its public position, the postal workers called upon other unions to join them in their defense of the right to work, and two days later, while Kruishank was being sentenced to fifteen years in prison, the sanitary engineers, in sympathy with the postal workers, walked off the job. As yet, no record has been unearthed about the collection of garbage in Johnson County. It well may be that no garbage was collected after that date. Dr. Sidey does have in his possession, however, several newspaper articles referring to the suicide of Iowa City's mayor, but that need not concern us here.

The widespread looting, encouraged by the lack of electricity and the lack of firm public leadership, increased in intensity. Four teenaged girls were wounded while trying to carry off color television sets from a Western Auto Store, and two cars were demolished in a wild chase across Macafee Bridge. The National Guard claimed the youngsters, carrying hand grenades, had fired first, and facts seem to substantiate that outlook. Still, the parents of the girls were scathing in their criticism of the Guard, and one of the parents.

Melvin Lindquist, went on a rampage of his own, tossing grenades and fire-bombs into the National Armory before taking his own life. The facts are not altogether clear at this point, confused by the breakdown in the mail service, but it appears that skirmishes were breaking out between Iowan citizens and members of the Guard, and that Cherokee and Calhoun counties, farther west in the state, were reporting troubles of their own. In addition to collecting, sorting, and delivering mail under dangerous circumstances, the National Guard was instructed to collect the garbage, and it was then that leaders of the Guard began to balk. In the face of an increased number of desertions, the Guard was in a state of mutiny, and the Pentagon threatened to send in the Marines to set things in order.

From the District of Columbia, the President of the former United States and the members of his Cabinet kept a watchful eye upon the rapidly deteriorating events. Worried that the civil mayhem would spread across the borders into Illinois and Missouri, the President's first concern was to keep the problem locally contained. After several all-night secret meetings with the Pentagon, he decided that Iowa should be surrounded and that no one would be allowed to cross that state's borders without permission of the Chief-of-Staff.

It is difficult to pinpoint definitely the straw that broke the camel's back, but the President's policy of containment brought blistering criticism from all quarters of the state, though Illinois, Missouri, and Nebraska all expressed gratitude at the President's firm stand. The two Senators from Iowa took to the airwaves and announced that unless Iowa's citizens were free to come and go as they please, Iowa would secede from the Union. War buffs hooted with delight, and statues of Jefferson Davis were resurrected and dusted off.

The President, however, refused to be intimidated. He knew his own mind and resolutely pointed out that the body count in Iowa

City alone exceeded 230, and that the end appeared nowhere in sight. The President, in front of the American people, broke down and openly wept, but that brought him no measure of sympathy from Iowans. Citizens, turned back from their own borders, cut from friends, family, and work in neighboring states, threatened all-out war and began to arm themselves. In his report, Dr. Sidey cites the turning point in the confrontation as being the rocket attack against the Air-Force Base in Mareirgo, an attack led by a right-wing group calling themselves the I.C.'s, Iowan Confederates. Other scholars, however, cite the sinking of the Battleship *Eldritch* in the Mississippi near Sabula. Information upon these two incidents is lacking, but whatever the turning point was, the end came swiftly and painfully.

On February 14th, the President met with his Joint Chiefs-of-Staff to bring the matter to a head. In the recording of the votes, as presented in Dr. Sidey's report, there were six votes in favor of "nuking" Iowa, no votes opposed, and two abstentions. The abstentions were from those present who had friends and relatives in the Disaster Area, as it was characteristically and euphemistically categorized by the press. In his presentation of the question, the President, who was an ex-naval officer, was tragically eloquent about the sinking of the *Eldritch*, and he is quoted as saying, "If we don't draw the line here, we might soon lose Ohio, Missouri, Nebraska. Why the entire Midwest might fall as an innocent victim to chaos! Fight fire with fire, gentlemen. I hate this decision as much as you, but the history of the whole free world rides with us. I say nuke them!"

And nuke them they did. Iowa was bombed back to the Stone Age, as the saying goes, or went. Perhaps if Congress had been consulted beforehand, the destruction of Iowa might have been avoided, or if not avoided, at least handled in a more humane manner, but time was of the essence and the matter was too crucial to be opened to public debate.

And thus the history of Iowa as a small part of the former United States was brought to a close. In subsequent press conferences, the President denied he had any knowledge of the affair. His subordinates were blamed for allowing matters to get out of hand. Alas, the public was handicapped in investigating the matter, for all information pertaining to the nuclear bombing was highly sensitive and had to be destroyed "for the good of the union."

Whether George Kruishank was among the six or seven survivors is impossible to say. The final Kruishank document in Dr. Sidey's possession is a crude homemade Valentine, perhaps meant for his sister who lived in Sioux City. It consists only of a red heart with the words "Be My Valentine" scrawled in childish letters. It was never mailed.

The Woman Who Wrote *King Lear*

⁓

The issue at hand is the authorship of *King Lear*. After maintaining my silence for nearly sixty years, and being of sound mind but of rapidly failing body, I, Muriel B. Hopkins, now nearing 85 years of age, have decided to set down, to the best of my ability, the truth of the matter. The time has come to unfold what plighted cunning has kept hidden. Many a critic has noted that the structure of *King Lear* differs significantly from the other Shakespearian tragedies, but none knows the reason as well as I. In 1605, I myself wrote *King Lear*.

To place you, dear reader, into a proper frame of reference, I shall have to transport you back to Boston, Massachusetts, in the year 1921. What a lovely city it was then, and not plagued by so much of the violence that I now read in the daily newspapers. My fiancé, the great love of my life, had been killed in the Great War, and so, retreating from the world, I embarked upon a life, not unlike my brothers, of research and teaching. I entered Radcliff College and collected materials for a thesis on the Imagery of Light and Darkness in Shakespeare's Tragedies. Shakespeare had been a great comfort to me during my dark time, and so it was only natural that I should study his works in depth. To finance my studies, not willing to be a further burden to my parents, I took a teaching position at the Emerson School for Girls. Thus I found myself, at the not-so-tender age of twenty-four, embarked upon a career of teaching and research.

I know that I repeat myself, but my mind is not all that it used to be, and it has been years since I have turned my hand to any sustained piece of writing, not counting a few long letters to my brother Jack and one item for the *Radcliff Alumnae Bulletin.* A tardiness in my nature has left much of this history unspoken 'til now.

I remain to myself, my brother Jack having died eight years ago, and I have banished all mirrors from my room. But I feel I can say, without displaying more vanity in the matter than is warranted, that at 24, 1 was a handsome woman, with long black hair that reached down to my waist, dark brown eyes that carried with them certain gleams of mischief, a trim figure, a well-turned ankle, a complexion clear and pale. I was fond of music, long dinners, good books, and quiet walks. In spite of a heart maimed by the world, I had heard myself proclaimed happy, and I enjoyed my students.

During my first year of teaching, I had taken lodging with a Mrs. Harriet Stanley, a close friend of my father's. Mrs. Stanley maintained proper lodgings (for females only) on Commonwealth Avenue. Thus, it was only a short walk for me from my nicely furnished set of rooms to the Emerson School for Girls. I confess that l was quite headstrong in those days, but at least teaching was a respectable refuge, especially for a woman destined to remain an old maid. At least that is how my parents and my brothers viewed my plight. I didn't view it quite that way. I had had one great love in my life and memories of that would fill the rest of my days. Of course, it was a different world then. In those days, a woman of the ripe old age of 24 without a husband to guide her was to be as much pitied as to be scorned. A good woman's fortune may grow out at heels. [??]

Not that I did not have suitors, you understand. There was always some nice young man turning up in Mrs. Stanley's doorsteps, some friend of my brothers' bearing a bouquet of flowers and small-talk, some dull-eyed divinity student asking me to accompany him to church on Sundays, or some brash veteran of the Great War wanting to bear me off to dinner or to some theatrical event.

I was not unmindful of these courtesies, nor was I unflattered by these attentions, but of all the suitors I had, none caught my fancy. My heart was elsewhere, and all of them, even the elderly ones, seemed so immature. A few could tell why one's nose stands in the middle of one's face, but only a few. The rest had but one thought—to sit in a darkened parlor and to spark. *Spark?* Do the young people of our day use such a term? I doubt it.

I haven't talked to anyone young in so long that I have really fallen out of touch with the modern generation. But from what have read, I conclude that they are thankless children all.

I do keep getting away from my subject, don't I? I shall return post-haste to the issue at hand: One Sunday evening while I was sitting at my desk, preparing my lessons for the following week, Mrs. Stanley rapped lightly upon my door.

I brushed Goneril—the cat—from my lap and stood up. My fingers were aching from so much writing and there was a slight pain in my lower back.

"What is it?" I asked.

"It's your brother, Miss Hopkins. He awaits your presence in the front parlor."

"Brother? Which brother?"

"Jack."

I searched for my shawl and managed to locate it under the chair where Goneril had dragged it. It was not like Jack to pay an unexpected call upon me, especially on a Sunday evening when he was well aware that I had to teach the next morning. My first thought, quite naturally, was that some family disaster had taken place and that he was coming to fetch me home at once.

With my heart beating loudly against my ribs, I burst from my room and nearly ran down the stairs, overtaking my landlady and nearly knocking her off balance.

"Why really, Miss Hopkins!" she exclaimed. "Why really!"

I could see my brother, dressed in tweeds. He was pacing back and forth with his hands behind his back. Usually my brother was covered with automobile grease, for machinery was his passion and he was forever tinkering away at things, working on some grand invention or another; but he wasn't at all like that namby-pamby photographer in *The Wild Duck*, I can tell you that.

Jack was some six years younger than myself. He was the baby of the family, and since I was the only daughter, he and I had grown quite close. He was a handsome man, twenty-one years of age, with a ruddy complexion and a thatch of milk-blonde hair, so fair that it seemed to be transparent, which was one reason, I suppose, why my brother always wore a cap. Not a few of my schoolgirl chums had expressed interest in my brother's future, but Jack, alas, was quite shy with the ladies. He spent most of his waking days writing for science magazines and tinkering away in a basement laboratory in a small brownstone located in Watertown.

"Francine!" he exclaimed as I dashed into the parlour. (I must stop to explain: Jack, by way of teasing me, had taken to calling me Francine Bacon, a jest that I was not overly fond of.)

"What is it, Jack?" I threw my arms about him and kissed him. "Something has happened to Papa. I know it."

"Something has happened to Papa?" Jack asked. "Whatever do you mean?"

"I mean, that's why you are here, isn't it?"

"Get your wraps, Francine. We're off. I've completed my Time-Machine. You must see it at once."

"Your Time-Machine?" I wanted to show Jack all the support I could for his epoch-making work, but all I could think of were papers to be graded, lessons to be planned. "I would love to see, Jack, I really would, but I have my lessons. Can't you show me next Saturday when I can give it the attention it deserves?"

Jack looked crestfallen. "Lessons!" he cried. "Good God, woman, I come to you in the hot flush of triumph, and all you can think of is *lessons!*" I lowered my eyes to the worn carpet. Indeed, I felt ashamed of myself. "Come with me and I'll give you all the time you want," he continued, pacing back and forth frantically. "You'll have more time than you'll know what to do with."

"No one has that much time," I said.

"Well, I do," Jack said, pronouncing each word quite deliberately. "If you don't come with me this instant, you shall never see me again. I came here to bring you face to face with your hero. Shakespeare awaits you."

"Well, keep your voice down," I admonished. I certainly did not wish for Mrs. Stanley to overhear my brother's mad outburst. It was worse than I had feared. Too much solitude had driven my brother over the edge. A life devoted to machinery. That way madness lies. "Let me make certain that Goneril is fed and I'll be right back."

Jack stopped pacing and dropped into one of the numerous over-stuffed chairs that dotted Mrs. Stanley's apartment. He pulled on the ends of his long moustache. "Well, be quick about it, will you? You don't want to keep the Bard waiting."

I dashed up to my room, set out a saucer of cream for Goneril, thrust myself into my wraps, and bounded down the stairs, once again running into Mrs. Stanley, once again nearly knocking her over. "Why really!" Mrs. Stanley cried, "I don't understand what has gotten into you tonight, Miss Hopkins!"

I didn't explain. Jack hurried me into his runabout, and we drove off in such vehemence that I thought I would never catch my breath again. *O matter and impertinency mixed! Reason in madness!*

We did not say a word to one another. What could we say? He parked the runabout and fairly whisked down the backstairs into his garage, a garage that he had converted into a private laboratory. There were books everywhere and test tubes, and at the center of the workroom stood an eight-foot metal cylinder—steel, I imagined— surrounded by wires and lights and radio tubes of all shapes and sizes. The very presence of the object seemed to calm my brother's nerves. He opened a liquor cabinet and poured himself a drink. I studied the contraption as best I could, but at science I was a veritable dunce and could not make heads nor tails of Jack's workmanship.

"Very nice, Jack. It really is."

My words must have sounded quite feeble. Jack, with trembling hands, poured a second drink. I did not approve, but Jack was his own man now, and I was afraid of any violent outburst. It was not the first time I had seen Jack in such a state.

"To my Chronomobile," Jack said, raising his glass in a mock toast. "Just as automobiles take us from one end of the country to the other, my Chronomobile, as I so style its name, will allow its passengers to travel from one end of human history to another. And when you return from visiting the Bard, dear Sister, provided you don't return on the exact instant you leave, the immense journey shall have taken only a few moments from your all-too-busy life. Think what grand lessons you can prepare, my darling Francine, when you can go to the horse's mouth, so to speak."

"You're making fun of me, Jack."

"Am I? I'm sorry. Forgive me if I am wrong." He took me by my elbow and gently guided me toward the machine. Inside, on a gleaming dashboard, there were a hundred or so intricate dials winking at me. "Picking a year was difficult, but I hope you find 1605 to your liking. London, of course. Now if you will be seated. I shall fasten this watch about your wrist. The rest is child's play."

"It certainly is," I told him, making no effort to hide my annoyance.

"Trust me, Muriel, and don't be so skeptical. When have I ever done anything to harm you?"

I sat down on the velvet chair and allowed Jack to buckle the strap. My evening of study had been shattered, and so I decided to concentrate upon my brother's needs. I was disappointed that Jack had squandered so much energy and money upon an invention that never could work. My plan was to use the failure to bring my brother back to his senses.

"There is nothing to be frightened of," he said, and it was only a half-truth. I was not frightened for myself. I was frightened for Jack's sake. "Be sure to bring me back Shakespeare's autograph," he said, closing the door. I could hear some bolts being thrown into place. "And don't worry," my brother said. "When you're ready to return, all you have to do is press the red button on that gadget about your wrist. When I receive the signal, I'll bring you back. I've tried everything myself. I've crossed the Alps with Hannibal. I've sailed with Columbus."

I wanted to cry, but I held back my tears. I felt bound upon a wheel of fire, and if I had shown Jack my doubts, 1 know that my tears would have scalded my face like molten lead. I studied the face of the watch on my wrist. It was no watch. It was simply a dark crystal with the year 1921 blazing forth in red digits. If my brother had been a watch-maker how happy my whole family would have been.

I could see my brother starting some sort of machine. Perhaps it was a generator. All I remember was a great roaring sound, then a burst of light. I was on a wheel of fire. The vault of heaven cracked and I was gone forever. Was this the promised end? What images of horror stirred!

Perhaps I made up the whole journey, you say. Or perhaps it was a dream. Oh no, a thousand times no. I report only what actually happened. I have held back this long because I could not bear to have fools cross-examine me, mock my brother's genius, for genius it most assuredly was. My simple soul had been flung backward through time. How does one describe a journey where your body becomes a sieve; where you think you are moving but in reality the world moves through you; a journey that covers vast distances, but no distance; a journey that crosses centuries but takes only a few seconds or even milliseconds from your life. It was close to a feeling I had had when I heard Beethoven's Concerto in D, Opus 61, for the first time, remembering the very first time it had been played by some clown called Clement who had the audacity to play it upside down on only one string. The string that I played upon was taut and fine. My eyes were a heavy case. You understand better than I how the world goes, don't you? Prithee, away.

The world goes as fast as we can or dare think about it.

"*She is not well. Convey her to my tent.*"

When I opened my eyes, after the roar, after the lights, I peered up at a man who looked like Shakespeare looming over me, his foul breath upon my face. I gasped. "No, no, no. This is too hideous a trick, Jack."

"Ah, she is coming to the land of the living," a voice said.

"None too soon to suit my poor taste."

I tried to bring the world into focus. There was a large basket and a plain wood table, and on the table, a dozen or so, well, they looked like costumes piled at odd angles.

"No, no, no, *what?*" the voice asked. "And who is Jack?"

"We are all Jacks, every man jack of us," the other voice added with a chuckle.

"Where am I?"

"Why, you are in the tiring room of my theater. Overcrowding and the heat—you must have passed out. Burbage here found you and carried you to this room. A saintly man, Sir Burbage."

The fat actor scoffed. "I commend her to your hands, Will. I'm off to the Mermaid." He plucked a hat from the table and smoothed its feather and was gone. I was chagrined to watch the second man make his escape so easily, especially when I had so many questions to ask.

"In wisdom, I should ask your name," I said to the face before me. "Will?" The man nodded.

"William Shakespeare, at your service, Madame."

"Of course." My heart was a-flutter. I studied the figure. Indeed he looked exactly as I had expected him to look. The moustache, the short beard, the gray eyes. Exactly as the playwright had been pictured in numerous volumes in the Radcliffe Library. I glanced at the gadget upon my wrist. It still flashed 1921. I scrutinized the tiring room. My brother certainly would not have gone to so much trouble for a practical joke. My head was swimming. "Water. Could I have some water, please?"

"Water? Ah! Certainly." And then the Bard rushed out, only to return after a few moments with some water in a tankard. I thought at the time I should ask him to boil the liquid for me, but then realized it would be putting the poor man to too much trouble. I decided to take the plunge, a plunge that I feared would bring me all sorts of internal problems. As I reached for the tankard and touched Shakespeare's hands, all my idolatry rose to the surface. I gushed like a schoolgirl. I began to babble. If I had giggled I should not have been surprised. I told William how much I adored him and all his writings, how I had studied all his plays. Words spilled forth in an embarrassing waterfall, but I couldn't help myself. Shakespeare blushed, and, not knowing what to say to me, took my hands in his. At the far end of the room, logs in the fireplace crackled loudly.

"Especially *King Lear*," I stammered, attempting to catch my breath, attempting to stem the flow of idiotic words. I was tempted to place my hands over my mouth to prevent further foolishness from escaping. For my brother Jack's sake, I thought I should ask the Bard for his autograph, but, for a brief moment, my nerve failed me.

A gasp escaped from William's lips. He released my hands and sprang back as if I had threatened him with a knife. *King Lear*, Madame? Who told you about *King Lear*?"

"Why everybody knows about *King Lear*," I replied, astonished at the playwright's astonishment.

"But it's the play I'm working upon now," he cried out in anguish. "No one knows a thing about it."

"Of course, you're working upon it now," I said, attempting to correct my foolish error. I had forgotten where and when I was in the scheme of things. The limitations of time had quite escaped me. "But there have been rumors. Everyone says it is going to be your masterpiece."

"A masterpiece. Yes, of course. But . . ." He didn't finish his sentence. Like my brother Jack, who had made the dream of my life come true, William clasped his hands behind his back and paced the

123

tiring room. So many of the playwright's mannerisms reminded me of Jack.

"How far along are you with my favorite tragedy?" I asked.

"How dare I tell you!" he groaned, showing his hands with their palms toward the ceiling. "There are pirates everywhere."

"But I am no pirate. I've come a long long way just to speak with you. Whatever you tell me will not be repeated to anyone who would do you harm."

"Promise?"

"Promise." Outside the window of the tiring room, some dogs were barking and howling. William crossed to the window to quiet them.

When he turned back to me, he said, "The little dogs and all— Tray, Blanch, and Sweetheart—see how they bark at me."

I recognized the reference immediately. I thought that it was William's way of welcoming me into his confidence. "That's what Lear says to Edgar in Act Three," I said. I wanted him to know how closely I had studied his play.

William knitted his brows. "What are you talking about, woman?" He opened a wicker basket and brought forth a handful of foolscap covered with ink. "I can't have dogs on the stage. It's impossible. Out of the question. Lance had a dog on stage. It bit Will Kempe in the leg."

"But what about the bear in *The Winter's Tale*?"

William looked puzzled. "I don't know what you're talking about. Are you a witch? Have you come to my theater to bewitch me, cast a spell over me?"

I could tell that, in spite of my verbal blunders, he was attracted to me, and so I pressed my advantage. "No, no, please. I don't mean to cause you any problems."

"You have. Many problems."

"Sorry."

"You are forgiven."

"Perhaps you could just read me a short piece from the play, something you are working on. I would be forever in your debt."

William studied the pages in hand. He placed some down on the table. "I'm working on the scene where Edgar and Cordelia marry."

"What?" I was taken so off-guard that I stood up, spilling the tankard of water across the pages on the table. Ink began to run in all directions.

"Act IV! You've ruined Act IV!" William cried, trying to blot the pages. I was doing the same.

"I'm sorry," I said, using my dress as blotting material. "But if you are planning on marrying Cordelia off to Edgar, then perhaps it is just as well that these pages be lost to history."

"Who is writing this play? You or I?"

"You are, of course."

"Of course," he said, with a trace of ice creeping into his voice.

"But in Act One you have Cordelia married to the King of France. Is she a bigamist?"

"In *your* play she marries France. In *my* play she marries Edgar. She and Edgar are meant for each other."

"You're only saying that because you don't trust me!"

"I trust you," he exclaimed. "Why should I not trust you?"

I felt I was pushing the poor man too far, and so I decided to tell him about my brother's time-machine and how I had traveled back from the year 1921. After I finished my little speech, there was a stunned silence. "Well, I did wonder about your strange garb, but . . . . You mean to say that you know how my play is going to turn out, and I don't?" he asked incredulously.

"Well, I wouldn't quite put it that way," I said. I felt overtaken by a sudden chill. "All right," he announced, taking more papers from the basket, "I shall read you a speech I am working upon now. Edgar's father, Gloucester, is blind and he enters at the beginning of Act IV. He is led in by an old man. The Old Man says, "You cannot see your way," and then blind Gloucester says, "I have no way and therefore I want no eyes; I stumbled when I saw. Full oft 'tis seen, our means secure us, and our mere defects prove our commodities. . . ."

"Excuse me," I said, "but may I ask you a question?"

"By all means, my lovely witch who claims to travel across time, from the Future to Here."

I had hesitated to interrupt him, but I knew that William would understand. "That line you just read, *'Our means secure us, and our mere defects prove our commodities. . . .'*"

"Yes, what about it?"

"There have been numerous critical controversies over what you mean exactly."

"What do you mean, 'numerous critical controversies.'"

"Well, there are hundreds, perhaps thousands of people who make their living by explaining what you mean."

"What are you babbling about now, woman? The people in the pit understand what I mean easily enough."

"Some people think that *means* means *mean things*. Dr. Capell claims *mean* refers to the middle condition, and that the line you have just quoted seems to arise from this reflection in Gloucester that had he been a man in that station, he had escaped these calamities, and his defects, which are his want of fortune and title, had hitherto protected him from the machinations of wickedness and so proved his commodities."

Expressions of grief and physical pain commingled upon the Bard's face. "I don't understand a word you're saying," he said. "All I mean is that 'Our means secure us, and our mere defects prove our commodities.' If I had meant something else, I should have placed other phrases upon Gloucester's lips."

"Language changes."

"Even as I write it, it seems."

"A scholar named Knight," I continued, "feels that the word *means* is used in the common sense of resources, powers, capacities. Thus, the means such as we possess are our securities. Our defects thence prove advantages."

William rubbed his brow with his open hand and closed his eyes. "In other words," he said quietly, "I should strike out the word *commodities* and use the word *advantages*? Very well, hand me my goose-quill."

"Let's not be hasty, William," I warned him, frightened that he would actually blot a line upon my account.

"But if people don't understand what I mean. . . ." He allowed the remainder of the sentence to remain unfinished. Still, I knew what he meant.

"Perhaps it is the word *secure* that is the bothersome one," I suggested. "A scholar named White contends that *secure*, the way you use it here. . . ."

"But I haven't decided on using it yet," Shakespeare exclaimed, crossing out the word. My hand reached out to stay the scribbling of his quill.

"But you will, Will," I said. "You must."

"Never. No, no. Never. Our means procure us. . . ."

"White contends," I continued, attempting to keep Sweet William's labors in perspective. "that you use the word *secure* to mean 'rendered careless,' though of course that is the radical sense of the word."

"Radical!" Shakespeare stood up and struck his sweating forehead with the open palm of his hand. "I'll render him careless if ever I place my hands on the dog."

"I don't think you shall," I said, pushing the tankard toward him. "Would you like some water?"

The Bard shook his head while I consulted the notes I had brought forth from my purse. "I mean you do use the word *secure* in Act Two, Scene 2, line 184 of *Timon of Athens* in the sense of 'rendered careless.'"

"I do? I have no idea who *Timon of Athens* is."

"You do." I decided to sidestep the issue that *Timon of Athens* was not written until a few years after *Lear*. I could see that I was causing Shakespeare's brow to furrow. How much longer dare I try his patience?

"Hmmm."

I had been hoping that throughout the course of our conversation Sweet William would notice my thoroughness, my complete devotion to his work. "On the other hand, Moberly contends that 'secure us' means 'over-secure' as to have a secure fool."

"A secure fool? I don't understand that at all." Shakespeare sighed and turned back to his writing table. "I think I shall simply blot out these three lines. Then Gloucester will open the scene by saying, 'How now. Who's there?' Ah, yes, that's much better. Do you think, my lovely witch, that these four words will confuse anybody?"

"I don't think so. But the speech really belongs to the Old Man and not to Gloucester."

"I'll get rid of the Old Man then. I merely put him in because Burbage's brother needs work. Now if you will just remain silent while I write."

"Sorry." I bit my lower lip to hold buck my tears. I did not think he was spelling *Gloucester* correctly.

"I know what you want," Sweet William said, pointing his quill in my direction like a small dagger. "You want Gloucester's eyesight restored, and at the end of the play Lear will move in with Cordelia. Then everybody will live happily ever after. Is that what you want?"

I shook my head. "But that's what audiences in the 18th Century wanted. In fact, many of your plays were rewritten to have happy endings."

"My plays? Someone rewrote my plays?"

I should never have said anything about the 18th Century. I tried to bring him back to matters at hand. "Perhaps you meant, as it is in some editions, 'Our means *recuse* us!'"

"*Recuse* us?" Shakespeare wailed. "Enough! No more! I don't know what I meant anymore. If people can't understand what I say then I'm burning my play." With that, he brushed the pages from the small writing-table, brushed them right into the roaring fire.

"Oh no," I cried. "You mustn't take anything I say personally." I rushed to the fireplace, but the playwright stopped me.

"You'll only injure yourself," he said.

"But your words, your immortal words. They're going up in smoke."

"They don't seem to be my words anymore." With that he fled from the room and I never, alas, saw him again. I stood and watched the burning of *King Lear*, then I collapsed upon one of the oak tiring benches and broke down.

I don't know how long I wept, but it felt like hours. The fire had gone out, and when I pulled myself together, I sifted through the ashes trying to try to find a page or two to rescue. I found nothing. How could I return to the 20th Century and find no *King Lear* waiting? How could I explain it to the Radcliffe English Department?

I could never look another scholar in the face. Literary life would be bare and bleak. Not to mention that my own thesis on "The Imagery of Light and Darkness in Shakespeare's Plays" would be discredited. I would have to start all over again. At my age? And what about all the actors and actresses and directors who have built their reputations upon the play?

My head was splitting, but I realized that I could not live with such a blot upon my conscience. There was nothing for me to do but to write the play to the best of my ability and give it to William as a gift. It would not be the *King Lear* that William had intended to create, but even an inferior *Lear* would he better than none at all. I dragged myself toward the writing table and gathered together as many writing materials as I could find. Perhaps there would still be magic in the bard's quill. I took a deep breath, sat down, and dipped the quill into the homemade ink. I began at the beginning:

ACT ONE Scene 1. King Lear's Palace.
Enter Kent, Gloucester, and Edmund.

KENT: I thought the King had more affected the Duke of Albany than Cornwall.

Affected did not sound correct to my ear, but I plunged on, and soon I was inspired. I was on wings. The Muse attended me morning, noon, and night, as I restructured the play, tightened the plot, improved the ragged rhythms. At last, I managed, being close to nervous collapse, scrawled the final line, tied the manuscript in a ribbon, and delivered the work to Shakespeare's home. I attached a note, imploring his forgiveness and begging that he make use of my feeble efforts as he sought fit. Perhaps my handiwork would restore his company to favor and provide him with further revenues to continue his masterpieces.

More I could not do. I did it for love, and the accomplishment of the task brought some covering for my naked soul. I pressed the red button on the gadget about my wrist, and, in less time than it takes to tell about it, I was resting comfortably upon the velvet chair in Jack's basement. I told my brother everything, and pledged him to silence, begging him, not only for my sake but for the sake of all mankind, to destroy his invention and not allow any other human being to tamper with the workings of eternity. And so it happened. My brother, who died eight years ago, took the secret of his work to the grave. I, however, feel that I should like to possess at the end of my life not a gravestone but some small footnote in *Shakespeare's Collected Works*. I shall deliver these papers into the hands of my nurse. I hope she will not laugh at me. I cannot stand the laughter.

Give me your hand. Have you no more to say?

The Cat That Swallowed
Thomas Hardy's Heart

Sussex
January 17, 1928

Dear Margery:

I know you are starved for news from London. Now what do I imagine you asking? Dear Sister, when Thomas Hardy died, there was, of course, a huge turn-out of literary folk and their ilk (assuming, of course, that literary folk do have ilk) at Westminster Abbey. Edmund—the Gosse that laid the golden egg—was there. As was Galsworthy. And Kipling. And Shaw, etc. Anybody who was anybody, I suppose. And Thomas Hardy's body was there, of course, for what's a funeral without a body? That rhetorical question, I am happy to report, still flourishes.

What was missing, unfortunately, was Thomas Hardy's *heart.* By heart, I do not mean his literary works, nor do I insinuate anything symbolic. I mean his anatomical heart. I mean his real once-beating heart.

Before the body was to be cremated at Working, Hardy's family had requested that the novelist's heart (it was a poet's heart too) be removed. The plan was to bury it in the Hardy family plot at Stinsford in Dorset. But, as another poet said before Hardy, the best-laid plans of mice and men frequently go awry. Best-laid plans go someplace they shouldn't go, and Thomas Hardy's heart, as magnificent as it was, was swallowed by Uncle Chuzzle's orange cat. So help me, God!

Hardy's family is notorious for its carelessness, and it is not easy to keep track of something so bizarre and tempting as a human heart out of context. Rumor has it that Uncle Chuzzle's cat—the infamous Max (you know the one, the Manx who scratched you once when you tickled it under the chin)—climbed through a window during afternoon tea, leapt to the mantle, tipped over the tiny urn (carried lovingly to Stinson by Sir James Barrie), and swallowed Thomas Hardy's heart in two or three gulps. With no more than a gentle burp and not even a fare-thee-well, Max jumped from the fireplace, bounded across the room, leapt out the same window from whence he had arrived, and was gone. How Hardy's family reacted to the scene, I hesitate to even imagine. I daresay it was not a scene to warm the cockles of one's heart (or Thomas Hardy's heart, for that matter).

And just what are the 'cockles of the heart'? I keep meaning to look that information up, but you know how things are. A person never really gets around to things like that. There are always so many more important things cropping up. The more I think about it, the more amazing it is that anything gets done at all. It probably takes every ounce of your strength to curl up with these tattered pages (paper these days deteriorates so rapidly) and make your way from my humorous beginnings to these amazing ends. But we shall, as soon as I gather more information for God and country, plough on.

Your loving brother,
Martin

P. S. No need to respond. I know how busy you are with the children, and I am—in search of more information about this frightful business—off to Dorset, a week or so with Uncle Chuzzle and our good Aunt Clare. Pray for me!

* • *

Dorset
January 19, 1928

Dear Margery:

Be things as they may (and they usually are, since the gods cannot control Fate), and as I may have mentioned in my previous missle (missile? missal that misses all?) our family is now up to its ears in trouble.

Aunt and Uncle, maintaining rooms over their tiny chemist's shop and praying for a miracle to save them from debtor's prison (doesn't life sound so Dickensian when events get out of hand?), have come into possession of Thomas Hardy's blasted heart. Well, not quite his blasted heart. The cat that has Hardy's heart (or had it, since by now the heart has been well-digested (and, if you will excuse the modest vulgarity) excreted.

Hush. . . . In the litter box there may well be the heart of Hardy in one form or another. Hush! Are you laughing? Giggling? Putting your lily white hand to your mouth like a common schoolgirl? Shame on you. Such is the economy of the physical world that nothing in Nature can be completely created nor destroyed, except perhaps literature and other works of art that fall into the hands of dolts, ignoramuses, blithering idiots, editors of literary journals, etc., etc.

Need I add, since you are well aware of the characters of our beloved Aunt and Uncle (such characters they are; they should be in somebody's novel), this concerned pair have carefully collected every bit of Max's stool they could lay their gloved hands to? "Might need this in court," Uncle Chuzzle says, displaying his prizes. "If push comes to shove, we shall need evidence that we did our best to preserve the heart of Thomas Hardy. Your Aunt and I raked through Max's litter box like harvesters in some kind of cranberry bog."

Dear sister, I think there shall be a great brouhaha in the courts over this flagrant cat-theft (dare I label it a cat-a-strophe?) and no doubt Aunt and Uncle will be ruined, and our good family name made the laughing stock of the nation. I suggest that you, Charles, and the children start packing immediately and hie thee to the next steamship to America. Americans don't take the theft of authors' hearts all that seriously, and I doubt if more than twenty of them in the hinterlands or outback or whatever they label their wild wild West have even *heard* of Hardy.

Flee . . . Flee . . . The game is up. It is not even afoot.

Your loving brother,
Martin

* • *

Dorset
January 22, 1928

Dearest Margery,

Of course I was only joking when I suggested that you flee the country. You have taken your husband's name. I doubt if the events of the day will affect you or the children directly. But the guilt here! Oh, my sister, you can cut it with a slotted spoon.

Strange events pile upon strange events. On the morning following the theft of Hardy's heart, Uncle Chuzzle (all 260 pounds of him! He has put on considerable weight since last you visited. At least five times a day, he sighs at me, "I wish Margery were here. We haven't seen her in ages"—quite a sight that is! And his hair, what is left of it, is snow white) dragged his portly and starched self downstairs to the chemist shop and there, piled neatly on the counter nearest the cash register were all manner of small articles—tooth powders, cough syrups, lozenges, button hooks, ointments, iodine bottles, bandages, etc.—all these sundries accompanied by a hand-written and unsigned note that read as follows:

Dear Sir,

I am ashamed to admit it, but over the past three or four years I have been coming into your shop and helping myself to the various articles which you see assembled before you.

Needless to say, my conscience troubles me greatly. I am no longer young (whether a man or woman I leave it to your imagination since I do not wish to give you any clue to my identity) and I should prepare to meet my Maker. As soon as I took the toothpowders home, I could not bring myself to use them. Thus, every article is being returned to you in a relatively pristine state. The boxes are still sealed; the canisters unopened; the lozenges unwrapped. I have wiped my fingerprints off each and every one of them, so there is no need for you to go to the authorities. I trust that this will remain a secret between you and myself. I beg your forgiveness. I throw myself upon your mercy.

Yours,

Well, Dear Sister, the letter has had our Uncle and Aunt in such a state. Such a state! Each blaming the other for lax (laxative) security in the shop, and both of them examining the letter for stylistic clues. The identity of the kleptomaniac must be secured, Uncle insists, whereas I try to temper his bluster with soothing aphorisms, proper Biblical quotations, and quiet allusions to the writings of Marx and Proudhon. Property is theft. Unfortunately, in our family, theft brings property.

For the past three hours, Uncle Chuzzle has done nothing but rock back and forth in that huge chair of his, pulling on his walrus-like moustache (I have been meaning to start a collection of moustache names. Wouldn't that be a lark? But, I have yet to get around to it), huffing and puffing and harrumphing, turning the note this way and that. Push has come to shove, he says. Next, he curses Max and threatens to put him to sleep. Then he curses the person who has been stealing him blind, as he puts it, though I doubt if the entire booty comes to more six-pound, ten. Modest thefts to say the least. Perhaps it is modest thefts that cut us most quickly to the heart? Pulling and pulling. That is Uncle Chuzzle in a nutshell, though there is no nutshell to properly hold such a frame.

I suggest that he scrutinize the piece of paper for the watermark, and trace the paper to its source. I read that in a book once. A mystery story, I believe. Or is every story a mystery these days? I ask him how many note-writers in the village are aware of the proper use of the semi-colon. The note is replete with semi-colons. As this letter is not;

Yours in the grip of confusion;
Your loving brother;
Martin

P. S. Thank you for the very charming edition of *Puss in Boots*. I shall present it to Max for Christmas.

* • *

Dorset
January 23, 1928

Dear Margery:

Now what do I imagine you asking, Dear Sister? I shall tell you what: The entire literary establishment is up in arms. Galsworthy, Gosse, Kipling, et. al (and they have all et) want Uncle Chuzzle incarcerated for life. Or, at the very least, beheaded in a public square. Everyone is quite distressed that Thomas Hardy's heart has been deprived of its proper resting place, neglecting, of course, the fact that his heart has found its proper resting place—at the center of his mighty novels! Or am I waxing too Romantic here? Too precious, no doubt. Still, Uncle Chuzzle has been in a profound pout for days. And Aunt Clare, no doubt influenced by the return of stolen merchandise to the Chemist shop, has written to the Postmaster to confess to reusing a two-pence stamp. The stamp, she said, arrived on an envelope posted from Piddlehinton, and the stamp had not been properly cancelled. Seeing a chance to save a bit of pin money, Aunt Clare steamed the stamp from the aforementioned envelope, affixed glue to its back, and reused it on a package she mailed to our Mother. This act of theft took place over a decade ago, and—don't laugh, Dear Sister—this past week Aunt Clare has decided to throw herself upon the mercy of the Court.

For the past four days, Aunt Clare has been lying on her bed in a darkened room, praying to God for forgiveness. She does not wish to go to prison for the theft of a stamp. She has refused to eat. "I can't stomach any more food," she had cried out. "The guilt is overwhelming." Naturally, Uncle Chuzzle, seeing himself being shipped off on some slave ship to Australia, has been of little comfort. He sits by her bed for hours at a time, saying, "No one is going to send you to prison, Clare, merely for reusing a postage stamp."

"I did wrong," Clare sighs.

"But was it such a *great* wrong?" Uncle Chuzzle asks her, tugging at his bicycle-bar moustaches. Names for moustaches. I really must get to that project someday.

"Dear Husband, I should never have done it. I knew it was a terrible thing to do. I knew it. Now I must pay the penalty."

"Push comes to Shove," he sighs.

Etc., etc.

Love,
Martin

* • *

Dorset
January 24, 1928

Dear Margery:

Just time for the briefest of notes.

Yesterday, Aunt Clare finally roused herself to go downstairs and work her shift in the shop. She twice broke down sobbing in front of her customers. To be sure, most persons thought she was suffering remorse for what Max had done to the future of literary anatomy. Little did they suspect that so much guilt and suffering was brought on only by a minuscule piece of paper and an eye-dropper of mucilage. Maybe it is the country air; breathing it in thins not the blood but the conscience. Consciences out this way seem so very very fragile. Not like those consciences that belong to staunch city folk.

Margery, I warn you: if you wish your children to remain in my good graces so that their educations might benefit from my generosity, do not allow my nieces and nephew to indulge in philately; I'd take grave-robbers to my bosom any day! Licking and gluing befuddles the mind.

Yours in the Land of the Guilty Conscience,
Martin.

* • *

Dorset
January 25, 1928

Dear Sister:

I know you have barely finished one epistle when another of mine, on inky legs, runs post-haste to your front door, but I wanted to apprise you of two silver linings in the cloud of uncertainty.

First, the Postmaster from London, no less, has written to Aunt Clare to forgive her of her misdemeanor. He suggests that she make things right by going to her local post-office, purchasing a new two-penny stamp, and having the postmaster cancel it. She is to send the cancelled stamp to the central offices in London, and the matter will be done with. Aunt Clare is saved! She shall not have to spend the rest of her years eating gruel in the prison house! Three cheers for English justice!

Second, Uncle Chuzzle has started to market Max's droppings. Yes, yes, Little paper jackets, nicely tied with red ribbon, filled with slightly fossilized cat dung. It's a grab-bag sale really, since it is unlikely that each example of cat excrement contains bits and pieces of Thomas Hardy's heart.

I suppose you think that I've gone mad or that Uncle Chuzzle has or that I am making the whole thing up, but I assure you, Dear Sister, I am merely relating the unvarnished Truth. People have been standing in line for hours to buy the packages. They go for two shillings per, and Uncle Chuzzle has visions of becoming rich. Very rich. It seems as if anybody who has had any contact at all with Thomas Hardy wants to carry, no matter how bizarre or distasteful the form, a bit of Literary History home with him or her.

The shop has been so filled to overflowing—a couple of scholars have in fact crossed the Channel—that I've had to go downstairs and lend a hand. "Get your grab-bag of Cat Droppings here!" I shout. "Each one may well contain a bit of Thomas Hardy's heart." Each bag is numbered and signed (by Uncle Chuzzle, Chemist) who attests to its authenticity. Everything in the bag comes from Max and Max only. Max is becoming a larger celebrity than Thomas Hardy himself. And the demand is overwhelming. I fear more good women and men want cat poop than they want *Return of the Native*. Or *Tess*.

Well, off I go downstairs to the Shop. It's my turn to pump up sales, though I doubt if any salesman has had an easier time of it. More anon.

Your loving brother,
Martin

* • *

Dorset
January 27, 1928

Dearest Margery:

The Hardy Family has taken exception to Uncle Chuzzle's "grab-bags" and has gotten its solicitor to request a restraining order or some such nonsense. But it's too late to do much good. Uncle and Aunt are rolling in riches.

I was wrong about the public not wanting copies of Hardy's novels. What Uncle Chuzzle has done (my God! What a mind of business!) has been to hire a photographer to take photographs of Max lying on top of each of the major novels. Uncle has had each photograph printed up as a postcard. The cards are selling at a rate of two or three hundred a day. Aunt Clare has placed ads in papers throughout England and America and the orders are pouring in. Pouring in! I have had to hang up my apron and take my turn at the writing desk. I shall have to make my escape soon, or I shall be enslaved for life. My solitary amusement is epistle writing.

As for the novels themselves, Uncle Chuzzle has ordered stacks of them, attached an appropriate card to each one, and then—are you ready for this, Dear Sister?—he has Max autograph (pawgraph) the title page of each one. You should see Uncle Chuzzle and Aunt

Clare. They come home each night, covered top to toe in ink. They look like a couple of Welsh miners! Bring on the private parts of Lawrence next, I should imagine. The cat will eat anything.

Forgive me, Margery, I grow too raucous, too rowdy, too indecent. But I am overwhelmed. My nervous system cannot stand the toil. The beloved Chemist Shop is no more; it will be a bookstore from now on.

What havoc has been wrought! I wish the Hardy Family had been clever enough to have kept their windows closed! You'd think they would have known better.

Your loving brother,
Martin

* • *

Sussex
June 13, 1928

Dear Margery:

Thank you for all the cards and letters. I am sorry that I have not been in any condition to respond. I think the Dorset Adventure (as Sir Arthur Conan Doyle might well label it) took more from my spirit than I dare admit.

I suppose that by now you have heard the sad news about the death of Max. I think the pressures of being a celebrity were too much for his heart (or hearts) to bear.

There had been some talk about having Max's body mummified and placed on display in the British Museum (If the family had done that to Thomas Hardy's body, what a load of trouble our own family would have been spared!), but, in the end, like most talk it came to nothing.

Two Sundays ago, Aunt Clare and Uncle Chuzzle held a memorial service for the cat, and thousands of mourners attended—more mourners, in fact, than attended the funeral of Hardy himself. Perhaps Uncle Chuzzle has informed you, but he and Aunt Clare had removed Max's heart. Aunt Clare wanted to keep it in an urn inside the bookshop, but three days ago, some miscreant swiped it. I wonder if it is the same thief who keeps pilfering novels and papers from the bookshop? Has someone reverted to their old ways?

The last is not a rhetorical question, though I understand that the rhetorical question still flourishes.

Now, I ask, what would anyone want with Max's heart?

Your loving brother,
Martin

* • *

The Interpretations of Dreams

Three days ago, after I had all but made up my mind to quit my job and go into the contracting business for myself, I turned on my radio to the Dream Network. You probably listen to that network yourself, especially to Lesley Hobbes' popular "Wake-Up Hour," where listeners call in with their dreams from the night before. It has gotten so that the "Wake-Up Hour" has now spilled over into a nearly all-day broadcast, but the Network refuses to change the program's name. "Wake-Up the Entire Day" sounds too silly. For a time, the program was sponsored by companies manufacturing sleeping pills. Today, the "Wake-Up Hour" is sponsored by microbreweries. In America, this comes under the heading of progress.

There has been some talk of transferring the show to television, but, alas, television is too emphatic for dreams, too matter of fact. Television sets rest in our living rooms and bedrooms waiting to be turned on. Radio is more conducive to the act of dreaming.

As for the content of the radio show, some of the dreams are real doozies, let me tell you. A good percentage of the dreamers out there should be locked away for life. Perhaps they already are.

Anyway, I was standing in the bathroom, shaving, humming "Questa a quella," staring at myself in the mirror, attempting to go through the mirror where all the realities are. So many things going on, inside myself and out! The caption on the newspaper photo reads: *During closing arguments yesterday, a defense attorney for O. J.*

Simpson, Barry Scheck, used his own sock to demonstrate a point he was making about a bloody sock. As I shaved, nicking myself on the cheek, I listened to America attempting to awaken from its latest racial nightmare—when Voltaire's voice weighed in with his ideas about "Somnambulists and Dreamers": "We must agree with Petronius's observation: *quidquidlu luce, tebebris agit.* I have known lawyers who have pleaded cases in their dreams, mathematicians who have solved problems, and poets who have composed verses. I have made some small verses myself, which are very passable."

Perhaps that was what happened to Los Angeles. The lawyers were pleading their cases in their dreams. *Peter Amelia, a law professor at the University of California at Los Angeles, said that Mr. Cochran might have gone too far both with his Hitler comparison and by essentially offering jurors a stark choice: Acquit Mr. Simpson or condone racism.* I sigh. The news is even invading the Dream Network. Simpson Simpson everywhere and not a drop to drink. I dry myself off, pull up my black suspenders, pick up the portable radio, and walk into the living room where my wife's friend, Madame Nemtchinova, was explaining Johnnie Cochran's remarks about the Holocaust. Madame Nemtchinova is an older woman, in her mid-sixties, with gray hair and a casual air about her. She was once the head of a private school in Paris, and, when she discusses the issues of the day she is very astute. I have never heard her call into the Dream Network, but perhaps she did at a time when I wasn't listening, though I am getting so addicted to the show that I can't begin to think of a time when I am not listening. I have even started to drink beer from microbreweries.

"'There was another man not too long ago who wanted to burn people,' Mr. Cochran said. 'People didn't care. People said, he's just a half-baked painter. This man, this scourge, became one of the worst people in the world—Adolf Hitler—because people didn't care, didn't try to stop him.'" My wife's friend lowers the newspaper and removes her reading glasses. Tied by a thick black ribbon, the glasses dangle to her ample bosom.

"Don't look at me," Christine says. "I'm certainly not going to defend Fuhrman."

My wife Christine, some twenty years younger than her friend, dressed in her black pants suit, is seated upon our dark blue couch. I say hello and glance out the picture window behind Christine's head. Christine was once a member of the Daighilev Russian Ballet, and one dance critic claimed she had the most beautiful legs in the world. Certainly that was one of the reasons I was so attracted to her. Even today, her legs are insured for a quarter of a million dollars, but the insurance company refuses to accept the risk in Turkey, the Balkan States, Austria, or Hungary. Don't ask me why. The world is getting more absurd everyday. No wonder we take refuge in our dreaming and then in telling our dreams to complete strangers so that they can comprehend our souls all the better. I would have more profound dreams if I had a more profound soul.

"As soon as anything terrible happens, we all drag up the name of Hitler," I say. "I don't see how it's relevant to this trial."

I kiss my wife perfunctorily upon her rouged cheek and say good morning to Madame Nemtchinova. She twirls her eyeglasses at me, and so I beat a hasty exit to the bedroom so I can finish dressing. I have to get down to the Charters Contracting Company as quickly as possible. Someone, most likely a disgruntled employee, has stolen a locomotive valued at nearly a million dollars. We have built all these strange contraptions—railroad trains, houses, classrooms, shopping malls, courtrooms, museums, sleep labs—and whenever we enter them, we become different people. I leave the bedroom door open so I can listen in on Madame Nemtchinova's lecture. It is getting so I cannot travel anywhere in the world without someone talking about the Simpson case. It has brought an entire world to a standstill. What does it say about us?

Johnnie Cochran has been widely vilified for comparing the trial of O. J. Simpson to the Holocaust. Madame Nemtchinova patiently explains whey he has been misinterpreted. "Mr. Fuhrman once said that he would like to place black people in a pile and burn them," Madame Nemtchinova says to Christine. Even from the bedroom, I can sense Christine's general impatience. Our obsession with the trial completely obscures the need for knowing the real from the false. Isn't that our true obsession—our need to know the real from the unreal? It is a great sin, I think, to wish for the real to become unreal, but what else can we do in the face of great tragedy?

That night Madame Nemtchinova's discussion leads to the following dream:

I am living in a basement under a bakery with twelve or thirteen other people, other families. My wife is captured and taken away by the Gestapo. As I approach her on the street, she discreetly shakes her head. We pass by as if we do not know each other. Another woman enters the cellar. She has gotten past the Gestapo. "Bullying the bullies," she says.

When I call that dream into the "Wake-Up Hour," the psychiatrists have a field day interpreting it. That's the way the Network runs. Dreams during the day, interpretations at night. I, myself, think it would run just as well the other way around.

They all become intrigued by the fact that it is my wife who gets taken away, and not the other woman. Why couldn't my dream be more centered upon marital happiness? And why are we living in a cellar under a bakery? Had I gone shopping at the local bakery during the day of Madame Nemtchinova's visit?

We go round and round, but the truth is very difficult to arrive at. Not only do we no longer trust our dreams, we no longer place our trust in more concrete phenomena, photography, for example.

Case in point: On my way to work, I see a cover of *Scientific American* showing Marilyn Monroe dancing with Abraham Lincoln. It wasn't a dream. It was a computer manipulation of images. "Curiously enough," J. Huizinga has written, "photography with its thousands of images has often done disservice to our power to image the past. Our heads have become kaleidoscopes of pictures of everything on earth."

The distrust of images has invaded our dream world too. I hurry past The Middle Hour Bakery where twelve to thirteen families are living in the basement. Many citizens of our city know this to be a fact, but we do nothing. We do not turn them into the local authorities.

Another minor, a most trivial, incident to prove how difficult the Truth is to get at: Take, for instance, the casting of Hitchcock's film *The Paradine Case*, a film about a trial where the lawyer's obsession with his client obscures her guilt.

The lawyer in *The Paradine Case* was played by Gregory Peck, who because of his lack of an English accent, would have been better off playing a lawyer for O. J. Simpson, a person with whom all America has been obsessed with for some 474 days and counting. In any case, what is before us is the problem of casting the film version of Robert Hitchens' novel (Robert Hitchens—does anyone read him anymore?). According to Leonard J. Leff, in his book *Hitchcock and Selznick* (1987): "Perhaps anxious to impress potential transatlantic backers with his savvy, Hitchcock campaigned for either of the two Selznick conract players, Joseph Cotten or Gregory Peck."

In his biography, *Gregory Peck* (William Morrow, 1980), Michael Freedland, on the other hand, states that ". . . Hitchcock wanted Laurence Olivier to play the barrister. Selznick insisted on Peck—who was big enough box office to take any part and get away with it. . . ." Well, not quite. But that is another matter. So who is correct? Sometimes, as in the O. J. Simpson case, the more evidence that is thrown at us, the more difficult it becomes to see the woods for the trees (if I may invoke that trusty cliché), especially in the Forest of Bad Deeds. "What is Truth?" asked Pilate, jesting. It is he who stands before you.

A kaleidoscope of pictures of everything on earth. Now we begin finally to see. Today the sun is shining and the temperature is in the low 80's. Everything is as it should be, but I am oddly out of synch with Justice. If evidence can be so easily planted, who among us is safe? If DNA is not evidence, then what is? A message on my voice mail says I should call Detective Bowler. He's coming by my office.

I am alone in the house—Christine has gone shopping with Madame Nemtchinova, and in the evening the three of us will be off to the opera. I am beginning to think it would be easier if we just asked Madame Nemtchinova to move in with us. "The dancers come out from the inner rooms, and their merrymaking dominates the stage for a while," I read in *The Pocket Book of Great Operas*. I always have to read about the opera I am going to see, and I have to buy a libretto to take with me. Otherwise, I do not understand most of what is going on. That is true for other parts of my life as well. We should, at birth, be issued interpreters to explain to us what is going on. But that is what I should like to do. I should like my merrymaking to dominate the stage for a while. But what stage am I on?

I then look up from out the picture window down the street to where the village green is. Under the oak tree is a man in a white sheet. He has been shot in the chest. A policeman is bending over the corpse. A second man with a gun is running away. Two dogs are barking, retrievers who live behind the iron gate of the house next to ours. Near the wounded man and the policeman, one of my sons— Carey, ten years old—is jumping rope, chanting a song about a policeman: "Policeman, policeman, do your duty." What is Carey doing there, I ask myself. My second question is: Where is Mark? Mark is my twelve-year-old. He is nowhere to be seen. In a panic, I run out the front door, run toward the small park. I gather Carey in my arms, "What are you doing? Where is your brother?"

"I don't know," he says.

I look wildly around, but my other is son is missing.

"Didn't you come to the park together?"

"No," he says, shaking his head.

"Officer," I ask, "what's going on here?"

"Do you know a man named Vernon Parrington?"

"No." I say.

I wake up shaking. I am firmly convinced that there is a man somewhere in the city with the name of Vernon Parrington and that he is going to harm my eldest son.

I had fallen asleep with the radio on, listening to the Dream Network, of course. What else is there? For the first time in a great while, I have something of importance to share. Perhaps one of the millions of daily listeners will know someone named Vernon Parrington. Perhaps one of them is Vernon Parrington. A man named Hillman, I can't make out his first name, informs the listeners, "A dream is not made by something other elsewhere. Rather, the 'we' who search for the casual condition of the dream is himself such stuff as dreams."

No, I think, no! I leap out of bed and trot down the hall to where my sons are sleeping. I make certain that Carey and Mark are in the house and are safe. "Get up," I call to them. "You are going to be late for school."

And then, shamefaced, I realized it is not even 6:00 A.M.

At one o'clock I am standing in front of the radio in the executive offices of the contracting company I work for. I have been there a dozen years too long. Perhaps I have been in my life too long. Perhaps I should audition for the Dream Network. The secretaries have stopped their keyboarding (in the days of old, we called it typing, but now what we do is not typing exactly), and another woman—one I do not know by name but whom I have seen before, somewhere, vaguely I remember her—has wandered in to attend to the report. The foreman of the jury stumbles briefly over O. J. Simpson's first name—Orenthal. What kind of a name is that? One worthy to be trademarked evidently. I think Simpson will be found guilty. Detective Ernest Bowler, who once taught sociology at UCLA, is far more astute in these matters. Yesterday he told me that if the jury was out for only four hours, then the verdict must be Not Guilty. "Even if all the twelve members are agreed on the Guilty verdict," he insists, "that is not enough time to argue first- or second-degree counts." It turns out that he is right, although Simpson's own lawyer has pleaded with the jury not to rush to judgment.

The week before, a fellow employee had also predicted the outcome. How come I was the only human being in the dark? ". . . in violation of Penal Code 187A, a felony upon Nicole Brown Simpson, a human being." A human being.

A human being. How shall we conjure those words? Human beings connected to one another. What connections can I come up with that will somehow join my life to that of Orenthal Simpson's?

I know a man who actually talked with Buffalo Bill. Thus, I can forge connections with persons in history much easier than I can find a link to O. J. Simpson.

I own a Simpson football trading card, but that's as close as I can get. Every so often I get so frustrated over my job that I have to walk out and buy myself an expensive sports card. It keeps me sane. That is, if I am sane.

The secretaries change stations. Everyone is in a hurry to return to the Dream Network where connections are more obscure. "Another group of dreams," Sigmund Freud announces, "which may be described as typical are those containing the death of some loved relative—for instance, of a parent, of a brother or sister, or of a child." All our fears parade indecently before us.

Five minutes after the verdict is read by Judge Ito's law clerk, the Vice-President in charge of Public Relations calls me into her office. She and I are about the same age—fifty or so—and the verdict of Not Guilty has visibly shaken her. She is also white. She is also angry. We are living in a nation being ripped apart by racism. But the truth is difficult to get at. Helen, for that is her name, cites a scene from *Blow-Up*. A photograph is enlarged and enlarged and enlarged. The original scene is no longer visible. All we see are the grains of the photographic paper. That is what happens to evidence. We can no longer trust photography as evidence.

But should this woman or anyone for that matter assume the guilt of a person who has been found innocent by a jury of his peers?

"What are we going to do about the missing locomotive?" Helen asks. Her question seems to be almost an afterthought.

The missing locomotive is a huge annoyance and an expensive one. The insurance problems are going to keep me up nights.

I counter Helen's question with a question: "Do you know anyone named Vernon Parrington?"

Helen turns back to her computer. "Vernon Parrington? No," she says. "The name does not ring a bell."

When I return to my office, Detectives Bowler and Wilson are standing in front of my desk. Bowler is an old friend. He would still be teaching sociology but he became involved with one of his students, a young man. It was many years ago. The radio says, "In dreams, when separated, the activities of the body . . . ," I turn it off.

Between the two detectives stands a disheveled black man, about fifty years old and over six feet tall, his black hair drawn back into a pony tail. He wears a long tan raincoat with torn pockets and a matching belt that has been pulled out from the loops and hangs forlornly down. He is as awkward as he is dirty.

"Who is this?" I ask my friend Bowler, offering him and his partner cigarettes, which they take eagerly. My office must be one of the few places in California where a person can smoke without being harassed.

"Here's the man who stole your company's locomotive," Wilson says. Wilson is the younger of the two detectives. Only in his mid-thirties. "You recognize him?"

I look into the black man's face. "No," I say, then settle onto the leather chair behind my desk. I wish to appear as official as possible. The two detectives, in plain clothes, remain standing. Their suspect stands between them with his hands cuffed behind his back. I was hoping the culprit would be white. Now the racial division of our city will once again widen.

151

"What's your name?" I ask him.

He looks me straight in the face, but doesn't speak. "Avenel," Detective Wilson says. "Luis Avenel. He lives on Parrington Avenue."

The name of course, takes me by surprise. "Parrington Avenue? Where's that?"

"Not one of your better sections of Oceanside," my friend says. "You'd have no reason to go out there."

The prisoner says nothing. Then Bowler reaches behind the man and presses his lit cigarette onto the back of the man's hand. A ballpoint pen drops to the carpet.

"What's that about?" I ask.

Bowler picks up a 29-cent ballpoint pen and carefully lays it upon my desk. "He was trying to pick the lock of his handcuffs with that."

"Would it work?"

"It's been known to happen," Wilson says. He pulls a small spiral notebook out of his coat pocket.

"You're not very smart," I tell the prisoner.

"You can say that again," Wilson says. He flips a few pages from his notebook and reads: "The suspect stole a fifty-ton locomotive from the Charters Round House at Clovis and Vine Streets last Friday night while its crew members were having supper at Denny's. The suspect ran the locomotive onto the main line and then jumped off. The engine, running at fifty-five miles per hour, went about four miles, speeding over crossings and endangering motorists and buses, until it reached Fairbanks Court in Ventura, where it collided with a freight train. Patrick Merrimack, the engineer of the freight train, was taken to Saint John's Hospital. He is listed as being in serious but stable condition."

As he reads from his notes, Wilson's head keeps bobbing up and down, like one of those little toy ducks you see on the edge of a pan of water, and after every ten or twelve words he suddenly gasps for air. Hollywood be damned. There was no way he was going to be a movie star.

"What's the condition of the train?" I ask, as if I don't have a good idea what the answer will be. The man named Luis Avenel—if that were indeed his real name (suppose it had been Vernon Parrington? What would have I done then? Leapt across the desk and throttled him?)—keeps his head down, but it appears to me that his eyes are fixed upon the ballpoint pen on my desk.

"Demolished," Bowler says. "You might salvage some of the parts."

"The freight train too," Wilson adds. Wilson is a sad-faced chap with green eyes. He barely reaches to Bowler's shoulders. I wonder what kind of a team they make. A dynamic duo?

"Why did you do it?" I ask Avenel.

"I did it for O. J.," he says slowly.

"Yeah, yeah," Bowler says, lightly pushing the prisoner toward Wilson. Wilson pushes him back. "Every Black in California wants to do something for O. J. Isn't it enough to set him free?"

"I was walking in my sleep," he says, defiantly, nearly spitting out the words.

"Mostly he was drunk," Wilson says.

"I can believe that," I tell him.

"Your kids want an iguana?" Bowler asks me.

"An iguana?" Now what's he talking about? I glance at the radio on my window sill to see if I had left it on by mistake.

"Before he stole the locomotive, he drank himself blotto, walked into a pet store, and bought himself an iguana. Don't ask me why," Wilson says, looking at the suspect.

"Good thing he didn't get himself tattooed," Bowler adds. "That often happens when a man like him gets drunk. He's got a lot of tattoos on him already. Want to look?"

"No, thanks," I say. "Besides I think the iguana belongs to the Mr. Avenel. I don't think the Venice Police Department can give away someone else's property."

"Oh, so its 'Mr. Avenel' now, is it? When did you two get to be so buddy buddy?" My friend looks a bit stung.

"I don't know him well enough to call him by his first name," I say, taking the ballpoint pen from the desk and sliding it into my top desk drawer.

"Call him Mr. Sambo, for all I care."

"Why did you buy the iguana?"

"I don't remember."

Wilson nods grimly toward my direction. "He doesn't want the iguana anymore. Right, *Mr. Avenel?*" He pronounces the last name mockingly. I become impatient to get everyone out of the office and to return to the world of dreaming.

"He can have it if he wants it," the black man says. He is speaking of me. "I don't have any use for it."

"Maybe you want to send it to O. J.?" Wilson says mockingly.

"Maybe I do," the suspect says.

"Here. Take a drag on this and calm yourself." Wilson pushes his cigarette into the black man's lips.

"I don't smoke," the black man mumbles.

"No. You merely steal trains and wreck them. A minor vice in the great scheme of things." Wilson pulls the cigarette out and crushes it into the iron ashtray on my desk. "I just wasted a good cigarette for nothing."

"It's not as if we're giving away evidence," Bowler says. "The iguana can't testify. Besides aren't you always telling me how much your sons want a pet?"

I sigh. Perhaps it will get me back in Bowler's good graces if I give in. The easiest way to hold on to people is to allow them to do you a favor.

"How much did he pay for it?" I ask.

"Forget it. You don't remember, do you?" Bowler asks the suspect, punching him roughly in the shoulder. "Do you?"

The suspect shakes his head. "No, I don't remember."

"My friend can have it then, huh?"

The suspect is silent. "Yeah, let him have it," he says.

"I'll bring it up to you," Bowler says. "It's in a cage. Mr. Avenel here gave him so much beer, he's probably drunk too."

"Thanks," I say, not exactly knowing if I mean it or not.

"We know a lot more about iguanas than we do about dinosaurs," Wilson says.

I look at him quizzically. I don't know what to make of that. We know a lot more about iguanas than we do about justice, I think.

Before I can think of something to say, Wilson marches the suspect out. I make sure the men are out of the room before I pull out several one hundred dollar bills and hand them to my friend. "Thanks for bringing the man in here first," I tell him.

"No problem," he says. "What are friends for?"

"Saves me a lot of work," I tell him. "You and Wilson write up your report and submit your expenses."

He pockets the money.

"You'll be very happy to know," he says, "the immigration people are closing down the bakery with all those illegal aliens in its cellar."

"Why should that make me happy?" I ask. "Why should it?"

He doesn't answer me. He just goes out. I turn back to the window with the radio on its sill to stare down into the parking lot. I get the feeling that I am seeing most of my life through windows.

Within ten minutes, there is a long cage on my desk, and deep inside there is an iguana. I call Christine and tell her that I shall have to skip "Rigoletto." I have to drive down to Fairbanks Court in Ventura to see the remains of the locomotive. It will be lying on its side like a destroyed dinosaur. Ah, I think. A connection.

"Are the boys home?" I ask.

"No. Their friend Vernon has tickets to the basketball game. But I told them to be home by ten. Vernon's parents will drive them home."

"I don't like it," I say. I write the name Vernon on my scratch pad five times. I had forgotten about the boy's friend named Vernon.

But his last name is Smith. What if it had been Parrington? What would I do? What would I do?

"I don't either," Christine says. "But what are we going to do?"

We exchange good-byes, with her asking me to try to join her and Madame Nemtchinova during the second act. She'll leave my ticket at the box-office.

I pull out the phone directory. There are three Vernon Parringtons listed. What should I do now? Go to their door and gun them down in cold blood? Why not? If I can afford expensive lawyers, I might get off. Of course, there was a man named Parrington who had written some history of ideas, a book I had been required to read at Oberlin. But that was a long time ago, and I have not thought of the book or its author since. I'm not even certain what his first name was, but I met a man once who bought Parrington's summer house in Vermont. There was even a car in the garage that came with it. A red Jaguar up on blocks.

It's not until after I hang up that I realize I had not told my wife about the iguana. Oh well, I think, let it be a surprise. The radio is back on. A man calls in to say that he had been dreaming. He had been standing at a lunch counter. There was a big wooden radio behind the counter. The man at the lunch counter said. "I am glad that my daughter is wearing dresses and getting away from leather, that old S&M crowd." The radio played a song: "The Vaccaro had a sombrero with three condoms in it, symbolizing the extent of his essential loneliness."

Essential loneliness. I like that. I could go on that show.

I carry the iguana, which I have started to call Parrington, out to my car, and start my drive to Fairbanks Court. Besides there is a woman out there I have been meaning to look up. She was once with the company, but that was three or four years ago. She may no longer remember me. And damn it, I want to be remembered.

It is getting dark, and Oxnard, under the smog, is getting dreamy. The lights of the city seem fainter than usual. The city drifts farther away from me. Highway 110 taking me somewhere.

Outside of Ventura, I stop at a small line of shops to buy some film for my Polaroid. I shall take some pictures of the locomotive. They may come in handy for evidence. I am certain my company will need them. It's not a question of insurance. We don't have any insurance on the locomotive itself, just on liability. That was expensive enough to buy. Our company will probably be liable for everything within fifty miles of the wreck. Strangers will stagger into the law courts complaining how the train wreck has destroyed their ability to sleep, to make love, to dream even.

What is strange, though, is that one of the bakeries in this line of white stucco stores is being used for a movie set.

I walk up to the roped-in area to take a look. After all, I am no different from any other star-struck southern Californian. Perhaps I keep hoping that some director will discover me and put me into the movies. Movies may be the last art form that provides us with images we are willing to give ourselves up to by our own free choice. Dreams give us no choice, and poetry nobody reads.

At the movie set, Martin Scorsese is directing some actors and actresses I do not recognize, although all the onlookers are *oohing* and *aahing*. I try to press myself closer to the action, which more than likely is going to be violent, but security guards turn me away. Three men covered with flour run out of the bakery. One falls to the concrete. My father once knew Robert DeNiro's father. A connection, I think. A connection that might matter. And one of my teachers at Oberlin was good friends with Stacy Keach's father. It is important to find some connectedness to the world, even in the most artificial of environments: a movie set, a mall, a marriage. Three men covered with flour run out of the bakery. The scene is over. It is filmed again. Then again.

I get bored and return to my car. Besides, I have an iguana to take care of. Why did I ever take the creature? Because I am no different than most people, I can't resist getting something for nothing. With the Polaroid film in my coat pocket, I climb in and turn on the radio. A voice says, "I am peering down into a miniature city." I ask myself: What would Fellini do with a set like this? There is an oval portrait of Fellini. Suddenly Fellini appears. He is climbing down a ladder. I fall to my knees. I cry out to him, "O Maestro," for I know he likes to be addressed as *Maestro*.

Well, who wouldn't want to be addressed as Maestro, I think, easing into the traffic. Christ, I am getting sick of cars and commuting and almost everything else in my life. Especially its lack of justice.

The radio plays. Kant says: "When he wakes up, his body is not associated with the ideas of his sleep, so that it cannot be a means of recalling this former state of thought to consciousness in such a way as to make it appear to belong to one and the same person. A confirmation of my idea of sound sleep is found in the activity of some who walk in their sleep, and who, in such a state, display more intelligence than usual, although in waking up they do not remember anything."

As for the iguana in its cage in the back seat, it appears to be sleeping, but what it is dreaming is anybody's guess.

In America, You Do Not Understand Your Life Unless You Understand the Movies

⁓

In America, it is impossible to understand your life unless you go to the movies. Movies are all around us; we couldn't escape them even if we wanted to. Movies are in the air we breathe, movies are in the food we eat (or dare not to eat), movies are in the very beds we sleep in—for we desire to make love like movie stars, lolling about in sexy lingerie in cavernous hotels. Movies grow by the side of the road, peep out between the wild flowers, withe-rod (*Viburnum dentatum*) of the honeysuckle family. In addition, I myself am not a member of the honeysuckle family. Like Jane Austen's older brother, my past life was put out to a wet-nurse and never invited home again.

Ellipsistic. In other words, I am given to the use of ellipses. . . . Movies even at the bottom of cereal boxes. No more Sky King rings. Or square inches of land in the Yukon. The other morning I reached all the way down to the bottom of a box of Iguana Flakes and pulled out a DVD of *King Kong.*(the 1930₂ version with Fay Wray). That giant ape is never far from my dreams. He was just misunderstood. No wonder I understand him so well. Anyway, as Mark Twain said, or might have said, or should have said: "Man is the only animal that makes movies, or needs to."

Even so, when I die, I shall petition, via my last will and testament, that my modest ashes be scattered across the front rows of abandoned movie palaces, or dabbed delicately upon the tender knees of tap-dancing Rockettes, or tapped gently into the pores of the sidewalk outside of Theater 80, St. Marks, where once, in my youth, when I had thought I would become the foremost movie scholar of the age, I viewed Jack Benny in the original and wonderful *To Be or Not To Be* (1942). And not the Mel Brooks remake (1983)! Originality is not all, but it is something, said Thomas Kyd to Shakespeare. Or was it Michael Kidd? One of them tap-dances.

NOT THE REMAKE (2010). *Not the Remake* should be silk-screened upon T-shirts for every member of the human race to wear. Unless of course Socrates is right and there is such a thing as reincarnation. Then we could legitimately wear the sign: THE REMAKE . . .

REINCARNATION. THE MOVIE (no date available). At the Roy and Niuta Titus theaters, 11 West 53rd Street (708-9490). A limited number of tickets are available to those who wish to return to earth as movie stars. Tickets must be applied for in person at the museum after 11:00 A.M. on the day of the Apocalypse.

Let the choir of St. Patrick's Cathedral, or the singers in every white-framed Baptist Church south of the *Mason-Dixon Line* (James Mason, Franklin W. Dixon), ring forth with the dialogue track of my favorite film—*Happy New Year* (the Claude LeLouch original, 1973, not the American remake). American producers think that all they have to do is find some hit European or Asian movie and recast it with Americans, and voila! You have a $500,000,000 gross on your hands. It rarely works, but lazy producers keep on trying. It's what passes for originality today.

E PLURIBUS UNUM will no longer appear on American coins and dollars. The new motto will be WE CAN DO IT AGAIN AND FOR MORE. Imitation is no longer the sincerest form of flattery; it is the only form of movie-making left open to the untried. And to the tried. Long after I am dead and buried my sons will be attending *Rocky CXII* and *Die Hard 798*. Let freedom ring as long as it is the freedom to do what has been done before.

Now that I am on the subject of my death (and is there a subject of more interest to my inhibited self?), let me point out that no obituary of mine will monopolize the front pages of the New York *Times*. Ah, no. If you wish to seek out my life, you need read no further than the "In Brief" listings of *The New Yorker*. There, by putting together clue after miserable clue, you will be able to piece together (should you so desire, though for what reason I have no idea) my miserable, insufferable, largely boring life. I did not fight in any wars, inspired no great causes, promoted no martyrdoms. I did, however, see a lot of movies:

HE DOESN'T LIVE HERE ANYMORE (1975). A comedy of sorts. A forty-four-year-old man can't get himself a decent job. He buys a Saturday Night Special and guns down his employers who don't appreciate him. By planting bombs in the remainder tables and cartons of books being returned, he single-handedly wipes out the publishing industry (of Manhattan that is, if there is any publishing industry in Manhattan). Full of rage at the stupidities of the modem world, he climbs to the top of the Empire State Building and grabs unemployment checks out of the sky. He crushes the tiny pieces of paper in his ape-like fists. It stars Kris Kristofferson, who sings some endearing love lyrics: "Ash Wednesday"—"Because I do not hope to speak./ Because I do not hope,/ because I do not hope to write plays,/ because I do not hope to get published . . ." (*Olympia, Quad, March 26th in the year of our Lord.*)

THE BIG PARADE (1925). The titles of this overly sentimental love story read: "My first wife used to cry at parades. Her face would get puffy; her eyes start to tear. It was the sound of drums and flutes and piccolos, the memory of marches down small one-horse town streets." I myself have marched in one or two parades, because in 5th grade I was the captain of my safety patrol. I wore a white belt and blue badge. There was a special way of folding the belt so it could be packed away in a tiny space. The members of the patrol voted for two persons to go on a trip to Washington, D.C., where the safety patrol was holding its annual meeting. I came in third, the alternate. I wouldn't get to see the White House and the Capitol and the Library of Congress unless one of my underlings fell down and broke a leg, thus, it is easy to see that I was not the most popular kid in the school. It was probably the first time in the school's history that the captain wasn't chosen to take the trip, which was all right, because my parents couldn't afford to send me anyway.

The teacher who sponsored the patrol said I was too free when I talked to the teachers, that I was always joking around when I should have shown respect. No wonder a comedian like Rodney Dangerfield is so popular. What man, woman, or child ever gets the respect he or she deserves? And what can you say about a life whose highlight happened in 5th or 6th grade? I don't believe I was elected captain of anything else again. I did get to see Washington, though it wasn't worth fretting about. They play the same movies there that are shown in any other place. Movies are ubiquitous. There is no need to travel across the world to see them. Stars John Wayne, Wayne Newton, and Bo Derek. (*Cinema 5*).

THE BIG PARADE IS OVER (1986). A country goes to war in the Falkland Islands. It defeats the enemy. When the soldiers return, the generals and admirals get into a argument over who should march first in the parade. The soldiers start brawling. The brawl escalates. Before anything can be done, World War III breaks out and the country is bombed back into the Stone Age. Starring Montgomery Clift and Curtis Le May and Curtis Le June and June Havoc, which is another name for summer.

BRAZIL (1985). My father never made it to Brazil, but when I was six years old, he did go to Venezuela for six months. He went down there to work for an oil company. Capitalism wins out again. When my father finally returned—after sending us hand-drawn Christmas cards, scenes of South America drawn with colored pencils on plain white paper—I sat on my tiny bed with a dog-eared deck of cards. I was afraid to go out to meet him. Besides he had grown a mustache, and I had never seen him with a mustache before. My two-year-old sister was sleeping and there was a stranger in the house. The following day I was involved with a pick-up baseball game. When it was my turn to bat, my father mysteriously materialized upon the sidewalk to scrutinize my swing. I swung as hard as I could, but I struck out. The man behind the plate, the father of two of my friends asked me, "Who is that man?" "It's my father," I said. Even the catcher could sense that I had changed. Some people wear themselves out trying to hit home runs for their old man. (*Reviewed in our issue of 2/10/2075*).

THE COLOR PURPLE (1985). Did my grandmother have a purple dress? I cannot remember. But I do remember that she took me to see *Superman Vs. the Mole People* (1948?). And then she took me to see *Sitting Pretty* (1948) with Clifton Webb as Mr. Belvedere. And then she took me to see *Captain Horatio Hornblower* (1951). For some reason she liked *Hornblower*, though I have no idea why. She really had no special love for the sea or for ships. But the movie was in color and it did star Gregory Peck. I can still remember one scene very vividly, when Hornblower enters his bedroom and piles the bed with hats and other clothing. Isn't it strange that a child of seven or eight would remember that scene and not the exciting adventure ones?

It is possible to chart one's life by going over the movies one has seen. And the people one has shared one's experience with. Thus, the vicarious experience of killing and loving becomes muted, softened, not unlike the way the old-fashioned cinematographers would put Vaseline around the edges of their lenses to hide the wrinkles of movie stars. What I mean is that the experience of going to the movies with someone you care about is more important than the quality of any shadow tossed upon the wall. I can remember every movie that my parents and/or my grandmother took me to. And that means remembering a lot of movies, for when I was a baby my mother would place my bassinet in the back seat of our car and she would take me to drive-in movies. Before I could talk, the dialogue of a hundred grade-B movies played havoc with my sensibilities (*not reviewed by us*).

CENSOR WITH A STRANGER (1978). A committee on the board of a small-time library convenes to censor the books. A tremendous wrangle takes place over one of the books, a book bound in expensive red leather. The book is completely blank. Everyone sees in the book his or her own pornography. Pornography, the first bawdy-building course. As soon as a new technology is introduced, pornography takes over. Think of all the porn sites on the internet. Growing up in Hollywood, Florida, during the 1950's, I found it difficult to track down sex films. My adolescence was amazingly pure and safe, as compared to the lives of today's teenagers. Today, any child can walk into the house, pop in a videotape or a DVD, and see anything and everything. The 1950's were much tighter. In high school, my friends and I would have to drive twenty miles or so into Miami and find an Art Movie House playing some movie, any movie from Sweden. Swedish with English subtitles. Swedish with Arabic dubbing. Swedish with French title cards. What did we care? As long as it had a nude swimming scene (and every Swedish film of the 1950's did). We would sit through any kind of romantic drivel for a two-second shot of a naked breast. Pubic hair was difficult to glimpse in those Cold War years. And then we would ride home, congratulating ourselves upon our good taste, our sophistication. Many decades later a noted historian confessed to me that he would go to the local dime store and search paperbacks for the word *nipple*. My God we were a desperate generation! Still, while our other friends were sitting at home salivating in front of Ed Sullivan, we were out on the street, roaming the world, in search of Art. Art with a capital A. Art, which means to a Hollywood producer, taking a bath, having one's bank account reduced to rubble.

WOMAN WITH A PEACH (1962). The first pornographic film I ever saw (Alas! I can't remember the correct title!) and it was very tame, showed a nude woman, not more than nineteen and so thin that she would make Twiggy look like Arnold Schwarzenegger, standing before a full-length mirror. In her hand she had a ripe peach. She took a bite from the peach and then rubbed it over her breasts. The peach in fact was larger than one of her breasts, but the idea was there. It was an Art film! She took a few more bites from the peach and then continued rubbing it across her nubile flesh. The juices ran into crevices we were not allowed, in those days, to see. For weeks afterwards, my friends and I could not enter the fruit section of a supermarket without breaking up. Many hours were spent arguing which kind of peach she used. *Prunis persica* with its single carpelled pistil. She was a pistil-packing momma, all right. And whatever became of her, that nameless actress? Did she marry? Did she ever tell her husband about her indecent past? Why couldn't I crawl up on the screen and embrace her? After all, I had seen her in the nude. We had no secrets from one another. But that will come, no doubt—the freedom of the moviegoer to crawl up on the screen and become part of the action. Laser movies. (*Reviewed by the Pope who is infallible and cannot be questioned.*)

SEX FIX (1997). Hector Borenco's latest edition to laser cinema. In the movie, you get to embrace a hundred nude actresses. You can put your arms about them; you can press your lips to theirs. You can dance with them, fornicate to your heart's content. All in the privacy of your own media center. Also, by careful manipulation of your image bank, you will be able to change the cast to suit your whim. For example, do you want to make love to a laser image of Myrna Loy or Henry Fonda, or some combination thereof? It is now possible. It is now possible to remake any movie in Hollywood and any where else with whatever cast you choose. *See following listings.*

LAST TANGO IN PARIS (1972). Imagine Jack Nicholson playing an American named Paul. In an empty apartment in Paris he meets an attractive young woman played by young Julie Christie. Bernardo Bertolucci is still listed as the director, but if you so desire, you may cut in scenes from *She Wore a Yellow Ribbon,* and give credit to John Ford. In other words, the cinematic world is now the viewer's oyster. We can, through the aid of lasers and computer enhancement, draw upon an image data bank and we can become our own producers, directors, actors, scriptwriters, what we will. For the last few decades, movies belonged only to persons who had a lot of money. It once cost millions to produce films, but now it is possible, right in your own home, using a few video recorders, some inexpensive sound equipment, to make movies for only a few cents a day. And no longer shall you be limited to living actors and actresses. And yes, you can put yourself into the picture. Do you want to star in *Gone With the Wind* (1939)? Why not? Of course you can. Anyone can. YOUR LIFE IS CALLING. Take video head shots of yourself and your loved ones and simply replace the shots of Clark Gable and Vivien Leigh.

YOUR WITNESS (1950). Not reviewed by us. All around the world, people are making their own sex videos. The next step has to be up, or sideways.

GREAT EXPECTATIONS (1946). Like every other young man setting forth on the great adventure we call auditioning, I had furious and plenty Great Expectations about my life. For over three years I worked in the town library and read all the great books. I was in high school and on Friday nights my girlfriend would meet me after work and I would walk her home. Talk about old-fashioned out-of-date dates! Talk about nerdism raised to the 9th power. Once we sat in the library's stairwell as I read aloud Dylan Thomas's great poem, "Fern Hill." How exuberant I was! How much my heart was in my throat. How much I wanted to leap out of my skin and enter the precincts of the Immortals. I wanted to write poetry and plays and make movies and dazzle the Universe and tap-dance over the planets. How far did I get? I sit at home in the evenings with a dead larynx, my days of narrating documentary movies over, and like other commuters to *The Kiss of the Spider Woman* (1985), I cry in my beer, longing for the snows and shows of yesteryear (yes, darling, I am all years) but with the dearly bought knowledge that I have now.

But now? What is Now? It is unraveling at 24 frames per second. If you are on film, you can rewind and start over. You can fast forward to the good parts. Her name was A. She was tall and splendid, Behind the Lutheran Church, late at night, when God had gone home, I would remove her brassiere and kiss and fondle her breasts, and become the living embodiment of the young boy in Winesburg, Ohio. I doubt if a full-scale orgy starring Charlie's Angels could give me such delight now. I drank in desire until my high school glands were giddy, until I knew that God would come back. There was meaning to the universe, and it was desire, pure and simple. Purpose and desire. I would hold her in my arms and sometimes she would cry because her father was having affairs and he was running around town, and she wouldn't speak of this to anyone but me, and she and her mother didn't know what to do. But A did not trust men, and every once in a while she would remove her panties and we would lie together on the grass under the not-so-simple stars, while something unseen and orbiting was bearing all our lives away.

Two years later we returned from our respective colleges. Her sorority had given her a pair of black lace panties because her pledge-sisters thought I would enjoy seeing them. I did, but by that time I had fallen in love with someone else, with a woman who would eventually become my first wife, and so when A and I parted, A was crying, and, for the first time in her life, she called me after midnight, and was crying, and another summer had forgotten how to breathe. What did I want, she begged me to say. What *did* I want? *Quem quaeritis?* We had sat through so many movies together, my hand going up under her long skirt. (*Reviewed by somebody, but not by me.*)

THE SUMMER OF THE SEVENTEENTH DOLL (1959). And what a strange summer it had been. And not in Australia either. Every time I turn on the television set in the middle of the afternoon, when soap-operas are spread out against the sky, the situation comedies are dealing with the persistence of memory, going backward in time. On *Father Knows Best,* mother and father grow teary-eyed over their college's 25th reunion, where both of them long to dance with their old flames. The next afternoon I turn on the set and *My Three Sons* deals with the same theme. Fred MacMurray's high school girlfriend comes to town (from the class of 1931— Somewhere in L.A. the class of '31 is dragging its weary carcass out to the Le Brea Tar Pits to die) and MacMurray goes back to the old kissing grounds. Finally, the girlfriend refuses to meet him for supper, but sends him a letter instead. The letter says that she will not see him because she does not wish to disturb the past. She wants to preserve the original memories. She does not want to confront wrinkles, and blasted dreams. It is a subject that is so complex and so common that no one, with the possible exception of Proust, can do justice to it. But then it is difficult to imagine Proust at a sock-hop, waxing nostalgic over a high school dance. As for disturbing the past, it is one of the things I do best. It is what mankind does best. We disturb the past and call it the future. (*Reviewed by Hawking, Heisenberg, Einstein, et. al, but we are not certain where,*)

SPLENDOR IN THE GRASS (1961) and not marijuana either. Now playing just like My Life at Film Forum 1 and 2. *ADOLES-CENT LOVE* in capital letters. But was there such a longing for the immediate past before the invention of photography? I think not. It was photography that gave the world true nostalgia. Not memory, but a past that one can return to by turning the pages of an album or by screening home movies. Before photography the common man or woman (who could not afford a portrait) had no visual access to a previous self. High school yearbooks (now being replaced by videos and web-pages and blog sites) have added a great weight upon the human heart. Where previous generations had no choice but to let the past go hang itself, the modern world has hung the past. Where do we store all those images of bygone selves and years?

Ourselves as children. Ourselves as newlyweds honeymooning by a Niagara of lost feelings. Ourselves with children. With grand-children. What frustration to have the past so near and yet so far. Whereas Sartre saw Hell as being other people, it is also Hell to be confronted by our previous selves. It is Hell because we know all those previous selves. It is Hell because we know what all those pre-vious selves will become. HELL, THE MOVIE. (*Not reviewed by other people.*)

VIDEO CAMP ON THE HUDSON (1990). At the world's first sleepaway camp for the VCR generation, each child will be issued his or her own VCR and video camera. A complete library of films on video will be available. Children will play on Monday and record their activities. On Tuesday, they will sit and replay what they did on Monday.

CAMP VIDEO'S ACTIVITY SHEET:

8 A.M.	View Horror movie
10 A.M.	View swimming film
11 A.M.	View canoeing movie

NOON: View lunch
1 P.M.   View baseball movie
3 P.M.   View football movie
5 P.M.   Eye Exam
6 P.M.   View Dinner
7 P.M.   View Teenage Romance
9 P.M.   Watch replay of the entire day
10 P.M.   Lights Out.

LIGHTS OUT (1987). A man is haunted by a light bulb that is burning in the apartment across the way. Every night he lies in bed and sees that light burning. After twenty years, he finally gets up enough courage to search for the source of the light. He gets lost and winds up in the wrong apartment house. Try as he might, he cannot locate the source of the light. Starring Fred MacMurray, Robert Young and Mickey Rooney as young Tom Edison. Con Edison does the billing. (*Reviewed by Watts.*)

THE FULLNESS OF THE GODHEAD IN THE CITY OF THE DEAD (1999). *Quem quaertis.* On the road to Los Angeles, the city of angels, whose full name is Pueblo de Nuestra la Reina de Los Angeles de Porciuncula, where, like a wandering ghost, I search for something I have little hope of finding. Unlike the main character in LIGHTS OUT, I don't search for light, I search for enlightenment. In the city of the dead, stars perform in open concerts. Bogart, Gable, Chaplin, Mae West. Here the dead work the real time systems. Come up and see us some time. Elvis, James Dean, Douglas Fairbanks, Valentino, Marlon Brando, Madonna, Jack Nicholson, Carole Lombard. The new gods whose surly postures reign some 400 light years beyond our ordinary solar system in a mass of anonymity, under the constellation *Ursa Cinema*, we common inferior souls huddle in a square open to the light. The dead do more work now than they ever did. What did Mark Twain say? "I never envied anybody, but the dead. I always envy the dead." Yes, he really said that. *Quem quaeritis? Quo Vadis?* And so it finally happens: After twenty-five years, my high school love calls me. We haven't spoken or written for decades, but I recognize her voice right away. After a few minutes of finding out who is sleeping with whom, who has children, who doesn't, who has put on weight and who hasn't, and who has moved to another planet, we run out of things to say, and so we start talking about the movies. (*Not reviewed by us.*)

Like my father at the same age, I have grown a mustache.

Lee Harvey Oswald's Can Opener

On the restroom wall someone has written: *Marshall has recovered from his illness.* Underneath those immortal lines, Marshall himself has written: *Please forgive me. I didn't know what I was doing when I alienated all of my friends.* Okay, I said, I'm willing to forgive and forget. Forgive and forget. That's the name of the game, isn't it?

So who is Marshall, you might ask.

Marshall Atwood McMichael is a forty-three-year-old white-haired blue-eyed Brooklynite who looks the way an overweight John Kennedy might have looked at that age. A thick-headed 170-pound Irishman whom I met through a guy named Moe D,. Marshall sells can openers for a living.

What kind of a living can a person make selling can-openers? Don't ask. I don't sell can openers. I don't sell anything. My wife works. She repairs television sets for Zenith. I'm in hog heaven and I know it. If you can't have a rich wife, at least keep a working one. Who said that? Socrates? Gary Trudeau?

When I go back into the bar, Marshall asks, "Do you want to hear about can openers?" He's carrying some of his Kennedy memorabilia with him. A black book called *Crime of the Century: The Kennedy Assassination from a Historian's Perspective.* The guy is always lugging something around. That's what being a salesman means, I guess, always lugging something around.

"Of course," I say. I can't wait. Tell me all about can openers. I roll my eyes back into my head and make believe I'm swooning. What's there to say about can openers?

"There were cans a long time before there were openers," he says. "For years, people had to open cans with anything at hand. Stones. Knives. Hammers. Imagine the plight of being hungry and coming across a cache of canned food and yet having no way of opening the cans."

"Sounds like my life with women," I tell him.

"Everything sounds like your life with women," he says.

On the bar, Marshall has a copy of *The Dallas Morning News*, November 23, 1963. There it is in black and white, bold headlines:

KENNEDY SLAIN ON DALLAS STREET
* • *

Johnson becomes President
Pro-Communist Charged with Act

A sniper shot and killed John F. Kennedy on the streets of Dallas Friday. A 24-year-old pro-Communist who once tried to defect to Russia was charged with the murder shortly before midnight.

Kennedy was shot at about 12:20 P.M. Friday at the foot of Elm Street as the presidential car entered the approach to the triple underpass.

The President died in a sixth-floor surgery room at Parkland Hospital at 1:00 P.M., though doctors said there was no chance for him to live when he reached the hospital.

Within two hours Vice-President Lyndon Johnson was sworn in as the nation's 36th President inside the presidential plane before departing for Washington.

In a room-by-room search of the School Books Depository, police found the rifle hidden between stacks of basic readers on the 6th floor.

The basic text: See the President ride in a car. See the President greet the people. See the President wave his hat. See the President get shot Run, Spot, run. Run, Oswald, run. Run, Tippit, run.

Did I tell you that this guy Marshall is a nut about the Kennedy assassination? Naah. You're probably the kind of person who would rather hear about can openers. More power to you, because to hear Marshall talk about the Kennedy assassination and the Warren Commission and all the assorted and sordid conspiracies and cover-ups is enough to make you wish for the return of Warren G. Harding. It's tough on a person's stomach.

Marshall collects anything to do with Lee Harvey Oswald. Anything. You name it, he's got it. A bottle cap supposedly belonging to the soft drink bottle used by Oswald before he pulled the trigger. A blowup of Commission Exhibit No. 1031. A poster from the New American Fact-Finding Commission welcoming Mr. Kennedy to Dallas, "A city so disgraced by a liberal smear attempt that its citizens have just elected two more conservative Americans to public office." A paper, given to him by his friend Moe, torn from the UPI Teletype Machine from Dallas:

UPI A7N DA PRESIDENT KENNEDY
Dallas, Nov. 22 (UPI) Three shots were fired at President Kennedy's Motorcade today in downtown Dallas. J71234PCS

Marshall tells me he's got a framed picture of Marina Prusakovina Oswald hanging over his bed. He owns a 32-mm print of *War is Hell*, the movie that was playing at the movie theater where Oswald was captured.

* • *

Movie festival: Movies and history. See the movies that changed the course of American history. See the actual movie that John Dillinger was watching before he was gunned down by the F.B.I. See the actual movie that Lee Harvey Oswald was watching before Patrolman M. N. MacDonald and his fellow police officers moved in for the capture. See *Patton*, the movie Richard M. Nixon screened so frequently at the White House. Of course, Marshall's favorite movie is—you guessed it: the Zapruder film. He's got stills from that movie in a manila folder. Each still is carefully labeled. *Zapruder frame Z225. Kennedy reacts to wound.*

Stop reading my paper, Marshall says. Pay attention to what I'm telling you about can openers.

I don't want to hear about can openers, I tell him. I've got other things to think about.

Like what?

Things.

Just name one of those things, he shouts. Some of the other losers at the bar turn their heads. For all they know, Marshall is just reading an ordinary newspaper. As if Marshall would do anything ordinary.

"Tongues of giraffes!"

Nobody thinks about the tongues of giraffes! Okay, maybe zoo keepers and circus folk do. Two points for you.

I do.

Why?

Because giraffes use their tongues to clean their ears with and you most likely don't. Why don't you try it sometime?

I slam some change onto the bar and stomp out into the 42nd Street snow. In a few days it will be black like coal. Holy moly, I think. What is my fate in life? To hang around crackpots? Kooks? Idiots? No wonder Marshall drives all his friends crazy! Can openers, for God's sake!

* • *

"It was important to show the world that America is not a banana republic, where a government can be changed by conspiracy."—John J. McCloy

Ta-Dinnnng. About two in the morning, just as I am sitting in the fifth seat, third row for the year in the Texas Theater, the phone rings. This is it, I say, trying to pull a gun from my belt. MacDonald charges me. There's a scuffle and I manage to pull the trigger on the gun, but the gun does not *Ta-dinnnng* fire. God, sometimes cops are just lucky.

And sometimes they're not. Officer Tippet, et al.

"Yeah?" I hate getting calls at two in the morning. The ringing of the phone makes your heart stop. Some family disaster has taken place and you're on the receiving end. There's no way out.

"What are you doing?" Marshall's voice asks.

"Studying differential calculus. What else would I be doing at two o'clock in the morning?" Two o'clock in the morning is always someone's dark night of the soul. Or is it three o'clock in the morning?

Let the Dallas Cowboys cheerleaders debate that one.

"What do you know about can openers?"

"Marshall, I don't care what you wrote on the bathroom wall. You're still crazy and you're still alienating your friends."

"Sorry," he says. "Go back to sleep."

"No, No, No. I'm up now. I pick up the small alarm clock and try to shake some morning back into it. "I know something about can openers," I tell him. "I saw Jackie Gleason try to sell one on television the other night. He and Ed Norton. He was the Chef of the Future and he got stage fright and tongue-tied and he and Norton ended up destroying the set. It's perhaps the funniest six or seven minutes in the history of television. Is that what you want to know?"

There's a long pause at the end of the line. Marshall lives in a one-room cell in the St. Francis Hotel. His room is a collection of black garbage bags. Each garbage bag is lettered and numbered. What's inside? All that Lee Harvey Oswald memorabilia that I've been telling you about. I mean, he's a demented librarian, referencing and cross-referencing dead particles of history. Or not even history. Trivia, call it. Or flotsam and jetsam. The *Atlantic Monthly* for July 1973, for example, where Lyndon Johnson was quoted as saying, "I never believed that Oswald acted alone, although I can accept that he pulled the trigger."

"It tells me more about television than it does about can openers."

"I know," I tell him, my life settling into a vague gray. By now I'm sitting up in bed, trying to find my slippers. The green ones. My wife is a redhead. So are most of my girlfriends. For some reason, redheads are crazy about the color green. Green shoes. Green underwear. Green contact lenses. The roaches have made off with them. My slippers I mean. $415 a month for a studio and I feel like a man condemned to Alcatraz. Anyway, this is just a place I use when I'm in town. Four or five guys I know, gamblers all, have chipped in for it. One of them, Moe D., lost $85,000 on the Super Bowl last year. I'm having trouble getting my share of the rent check from him. Still, this little apartment is one of the few investments I trust. And it's a good place to bring women, not that I have a woman with me now. I've got woman trouble like you wouldn't believe.

Good thing my wife is back in Saratoga. Otherwise there would be hell to pay. She hates it when my friends call at two in the morning. She particularly hates it when Marshall calls at two in the morning. She particularly hates Marshall. I guess most people do. He's obsessive. His constant talk about the Kennedy assassination alienates everybody.

"I know a place in Texas, a small family-run museum that contains a can opener once owned by Lee Harvey Oswald," Marshall says.

How shall I describe his voice? It is high-pitched, nasal. A cross between a desperate automobile salesman and a Latin teacher dragging her fingernails down the blackboard. *E Pluribus Unum.* It's nothing any ordinary human wants to hear at two in the morning. There are not many things I want to hear at two in the morning. Unless it's related to sex. And what's related to sex? Not can openers. "I have a chance to get it," he adds.

"I'm happy for you," I tell him, dangling my legs over the side of the bed, into roach paradise, listening to the sounds of traffic. For twenty years I have lived in New York, and it's the sound of traffic late at night I find most soothing. Knowledge that somebody, no matter the lateness of the hour, is always going somewhere. Then the sanitation trucks in the early morning. The ritual of it all.

"I'm ecstatic," I tell him. "Want me to dash outside in my pajamas and dance in the streets? I find a cigarette and light it. I should give up smoking, but I'm too old to give up small, inexpensive pleasures, especially at a time when all the big and expensive pleasures are being torn away. My wife says cities are not a good place to live. She would rather be in the country selling crystals to hail-starved nature lovers and defrocked farmers. According to her, the secret of life is in crystals. She even had funny little cards made up—blue cards with red borders. Crystals to solve the problems of life. Just what I need. A magic crystal to solve the problems of life.

"No you're not. You think I'm a raving lunatic."

"No, I don't," I lied. "Where are you calling from?"

"I'm at home. Where else would I be?"

"Okay. Okay. Okay. Okay. What do you want from me?"

"Five grand. Can you lend me five grand?"

I fall back on my bed and allow circles of smoke to halo toward the ceiling. With any luck I shall fall asleep with the cigarette in my hand and then the bed will catch fire and I'll die.

"Hello? You still there?"

"Five grand for a can opener?" 1 ask.

"Not just for the can opener," he says. "I've got to go out there and bring it hack?"

"Can't they just mail it to you?"

"They don't want to sell it?'

"If they don't want to sell it, how are you going to get it?"

"Just five grand?'

"I love the way you say that: *Just* five grand. Why don't you sell some of your Lee Harvey Oswald collection?"

"Why would I want to sell it when I want to add to it?"

"The duplicates," I tell him. "You must have a lot of duplicates. How many copies of *The Dallas Morning News* do you need? How many framed photos of Jack Ruby?"

"If you think I'm so crazy, why don't you read some of the books I've got?"

"Like what?"

"How about *The Case Against Lyndon B. Johnson in the Assassination of President Kennedy*? Published in Munich. Or you could read Stanley Marks' book, *Murder Most Foul! The Conspiracy that Murdered President Kennedy: 975 Questions and Answers. 1967.*"

"Well, I've got nothing better to do between now and the start of the Mets game. Send them over?"

"You crazy? I'm not going to send them over. You come over here. You've got to read them here?"

Pause. I feel like a drowning man. Whenever a friend asks me for money, I feel my entire life flashing before my eyes. Neither a borrower nor a lender be. Who said that? Nick the Greek? J.P. Morgan?

"Do 1 get the money or not?"

"No."

"Thanks?"

Pause.

"I'll lend you two?"

"I don't want two. I want five. I need five. I'll pay you five hundred interest in two weeks?"

"Seven-hundred-and-fifty interest in ten days?" My old man wasn't a bank clerk for nothing.

Pause.

"Okay."

"Okay. And if you don't, you die?"

"Sounds fair?"

He hangs up. I hang up. Click. Click. Life is like that. A series of small clicks.

I get dressed and go out to get some rye bread, baked beans, and corned beef. Those are three things that Nero Wolfe never allows to be served at his table. Aside from those three items, Nero Wolfe's chef Fritz Brenner has a free hand.

Now you know the kind of stuff I read.

2

Three weeks later I get my money. With interest. I have many bad things to say about Marshall, but at least he pays back what he borrows. Good thing, too, because I am getting clobbered betting the horses. Only an idiot bets the horses. But I've got to do something to keep from going crazy. The longer you live, the deeper you realize how the odds are very much against you. No wonder misbegotten and far-flung souls climb to the top of book depositories to do somebody else dirt, landing square in the history books, lolling about on the cusp of immortality. Good men die unnoticed, but scholars devote thousands upon thousands of pages to biographing and analyzing the villains. Murderers and killers and Cheap-Shot Harrys.

It's Marshall talking: The rifle found on the sixth floor of the Texas School Book Depository shortly after the assassination was a bolt-action, clip-fed military rifle. The rifle was about forty inches long and weighed eight pounds. There were markings on the rifle, including the words CAL. 6.5, meaning that the rifle was 6.5 millimeter. Other markings indicated that it was "Made in Italy," "Terni" and "Rocca." The serial number of the rifle used to kill the president was C2766. Thus, according to the sacred Warren Commission Report, the rifle was a 6.5 millimeter Mannlicher Carino military rifle.

"However," and now Marshall's high-pitched voice rises even further in excitement, "according to Stanley Marks' book, Deputy Sheriff Weitzman, who saw and found the rifle, signed on November 23, 1963, an affidavit which stated that the rifle he found was a 7.65 Mauser bolt-action equipped with a 4/18 scope with a thick brownish sling on it? So what became of that rifle? Was that the one used? Did it belong to someone else?"

Marshall, seated amid his black garbage bags like a broken-hearted Buddha, his hands uplifted toward the ceiling, asks "Doesn't that discrepancy bother you?"

"No," I tell him. "I believe the Warren Commission Report. And don't give me that stuff about Lyndon B. Johnson being implicated. That's garbage?"

"You don't want to know the truth?"

"Do you?"

"There was an eyewitness, a Dallas TV commentator, who claimed that he saw a rifle sticking out of the second floor of the Cal Tex Building?"

"What do you want me to do about it?" I shout.

"Doesn't it bother you that David Powers, a man who was an aide to President Kennedy and a passenger in the Dallas motorcade, said on television in Boston in May of 1976 that 'If the bullet that wounded the president was not the same bullet that wounded John Connolly—and I testified that it wasn't, and John Connolly testified that it wasn't—then there would have to be more than one assassin?"

"Who was it? You?"

"Stop being such a wiseass and listen to the facts for once?"

"I bet you have the tape, too?"

"I do. You want to see it?"

I shake my head. Life is too short. What does the world gain by beating so many dead horses? "Are Powers and Connolly experts on ballistics? My friend Moe, $85,000 in debt, knows more about ballistics than those two jokers. And in addition, even if I had the time and the interest, which I do not, I don't have the resources to investigate a crime that took place over twenty years ago. Our government has got a lock on it?"

"1 bet you think it was a federal crime?"

"I don't think anything?"

"Well, it wasn't. At the time of Kennedy's assassination, it was not a federal crime to the kill the President of the United States. Oswald's trial would have been under the jurisdiction of the State of Texas?"

"You know what I say?"

"What do you say?"

"I say take everything you have collected, drag it out to some open field and burn it?"

A look of anguish comes over Marshall's face. "Burn it?"

"Burn everything. Every chicken bone, every bottle cap, bottle opener."

"Can opener?" he says holding it into the air triumphantly. He owns Lee Harvey Oswald's can opener and so now he's special. He's entitled to his place in heaven. Just the way teenage adolescents— mixed-up, crazy, and sad—start after Nazi flags and helmets and crosses. I am on a roll. I grab a sheaf of music papers from his unmade bed. The whole room is unmade.

"Every little stinking thing. Every rotten book you own. Every piece of paper. Every weirdo letter." I thrust sheets of music papers under Marshall's nose. "What's this, for example?"

Marshall is startled by my vehemence. I'm sick and tired of every two-bit chicken-legged scrawny-necked no-brained psychopath taking up so much time and goodness from our lives. Pages and pages of history devoted to Lee Harvey Oswald and Guiteau and Hitler and whoever, people not worth spitting upon, not worth considering, not worth thinking about, not worthy of having so much attention heaped upon them, while good honest hard-working folk such as myself disappear into a great void. No wonder conspiracy theories are so popular. Life itself is a conspiracy, and as you get older you learn to trust fewer and fewer people. "What's this?" I repeat.

"It's an oratorio by some composer from Utah. A Mormon I think." Marshall takes the sheaf of music papers from my hand and begins to sing:

"I, Lee Harvey Oswald, do hereby request that my present citizenship in the United States of America be revoked.

"I have entered the Soviet Union for the express purpose of applying for citizenship in the Soviet Union, through the means of naturalization.

"My request for citizenship is now pending before the Supreme Soviet of the USSR.

"I take these steps for political reasons. My request for the revoking of my American Citizenship is made only after the longest and most serious consideration."

The late Fred Allen of radio fame once described his wife Portland's voice as the sound of "two slate pencils mating or a clarinet reed calling for help." That description could very well apply to Marshall's own singing voice. Not that what he was singing was melodic. What's wrong with melody? Why do people have to hang around juke boxes in bars to hear anything half pleasant?

"That's not worth saving either. Trash it. Trash everything. Let the dead bury the dead." I reach up to take down his framed picture of Marina Prusakovina Oswald.

"Leave it alone," he says.

There's something in his voice, harsh and cold, that stops me, warns me not to tamper. But since I am close to the picture I can see that it is autographed, inscribed: To Marshall, a friend in need. Marina.

"I am not a junk man," Marshall says, wiping his eyes. "I am a historian. I am collecting valuable evidence for the next generations?"

"Evidence of what?"

"The truth?"

Whenever I hear someone utter the word *truth*, I want to vomit. Everybody thinks they've got the handle on it.

"It makes me sick to my stomach," I tell him. "All you're doing is encouraging persons to murder."

Pause.

"How am I encouraging persons to murder?"

I've got him by the short hairs now. "By turning killers into valuable commodities. We exhibit their can openers and sell their toenail clippings. Magazine editors and publishers and reputable scholars come running when they hear rumors that Hitler left behind his diaries."

"Oswald was not Hitler."

"The principle is the same. We take persons who don't deserve to be remembered and we remember them beyond all decency."

"Maybe there is something to be learned from them."

"No. Nothing. Nothing. Nothing. It would be better if their names were blotted from history forever. We have nothing to learn from their putrid, empty, stinking souls. $20,000 for the diaries of Hitler is obscene. $5,000 for Lee Harvey Oswald's can opener is obscene."

Marshall shrugs, takes the can opener and wraps it carefully in clear plastic. He labels it and puts it on a shelf, his own private museum.

"It's what the market will bear," he says. "That's what the world adds up to. Market value. Why do you think millionaires run around grabbing up Van Gogh paintings for thirty million dollars at a clip? You think they love art?"

"If Oswald were alive today, he would have an agent, and the agent would be selling Oswald's life story to the movies and to television for millions of dollars." My voice drips with venom, rage, and self-loathing. "T-shirt manufacturers would hunger for Oswald's likeness. There would candy bars named after him. Thank God for Jack Ruby."

"Thank God for Jack Ruby," Marshall repeats softly, his voice like a clarinet reed, not entirely believing the words the way I do. In truth, his apartment has taken on an unpleasant odor, the odor of another life gone wrong. I head for the door. I'll bet on any horse that has the word *bullet* in its name. *To Marshall, a friend in need. Marina.* Indeed!

3

For six months I stay out of Marshall's way, and he stays out of mine. And then one morning, when I am back in town, working on a small job involving the fixing of a high school basketball game, I get a phone call at two in the morning. The blonde I've got with me nearly goes off the deep end. "Who in the hell is calling at this hour of the night?" I tell her to shut up in case it's my old lady calling from Saratoga. Saratoga, I think. What a town. There are days I miss the ponies so bad think I'm going to die.

"Has the F.B.I. visited you yet?" the voice on the other end asks, high-pitched, nasal. No need to guess who it is. No need to guess what anything is. Whatever happened to quiz shows? Remember when they were all the rage? My heart stops cold. I reach back and with my free hand I caress Lorraine's thighs. Has someone squealed about the basketball fix? Gotta play dumb, I guess. "No. No F.B.I.," I say. "Why should they knock upon my door?"

"Because they're after me," Marshall says.

"Why are they after you?" Lorraine tosses the naked covers back and walks to the bathroom. Holy moly. I'm getting too nakedly old. My naked heart can't take all the action. I need an older woman. Anybody but my old lady. Take my wife. Please! Who said that? I am sure it was John Mitchell. Who was deep throating whom?

"Because they say I wrote a letter to Senator Kennedy," Marshall says.

"They?"

"Who else?"

Pause. Whisper. "Someone has offered to kill Oswald's brother for him."

"What?"

Reaching for my cigarettes, I knock the green lamp over. I hear Lorraine turning on the shower. Why is she taking a shower? Women. They're all crazy.

"Can you meet me?"

"When?"

"Now. Kraft's coffee shop. 10th Avenue and 42nd Street. Hurry." Click. I am left holding another pound of silence. I hang up. Click. Click. Life is like that. A series of small clicks. Have I said that before? Then what hasn't been said before?

What am I supposed to do now? I've got a twenty-four-year-old woman in the shower. My wife is expecting me back in Saratoga tomorrow afternoon. I've got three basketball players to pay off. And Marshall's got the F.B.I. after him. Best to keep out of it, I think. He's got his problems and I've got mine. Lorraine returns pink and fresh and willing. Not exactly two slate pencils mating.

4

The next morning the newspapers are filled with it. Senator Kennedy has released Marshall's letter to the press. And there it is: Front page of the *Daily News*:

BROTHER FOR BROTHER (The letter is reproduced in all its childish and shaky handwriting.)

Dear Senator Kennedy:

As you are well aware, Lee Harvey Oswald has a brother named Robert. Because Lee shot your brother John, would it not be right that one of the Kennedys shot Robert? I know that because of your high public office you yourself cannot undertake such a hazardous assignment. However, because of my great admiration for your brother, 1 will be glad to do it. All I would ask is $50,000 in cash to be delivered to the above address within ten days.

I am certain you know that what 1 propose is the right thing to do. Eye for an eye, tooth for a tooth is the only real justice there is. Because of the rash act of Ruby, Lee Harvey Oswald is never brought to trial, and thus, America was deprived of the full truth of his undertaking, and you and your family have been deprived of justice.

I read the letter again and again. The inside pages point out that the letter is dated October 18th, the birthday of Lee Harvey Oswald.

Indeed there is a Robert L. Oswald, and he has probably suffered the way Edwin Booth was forced to suffer because of the mad acts of his brother. The parallels between the careers and deaths of Kennedy and Lincoln always made superior reading for connoisseurs of the weird.

Next I turn to the sports pages. The handicappers have picked a horse named Nixon's-the-One to win. A sucker bet if ever there was one.

Two days later, John Connolly gets the same letter. For a mere $35,000, Marshall offers to wound Robert Oswald.

A few more days pass. A plain white envelope arrives in the mail. Inside is a Xeroxed sheet that reads:

McCloy: The time is almost overdue for us to have a better perspective of the FBI investigation than we have now. We are so dependent on them for our facts.

Rankin: Part of our difficulty in regard to it is that they have no problem. They have decided that it is Oswald who committed the assassination; they have decided no one else is involved.

Russell: They have tried the case and reached a verdict on every aspect.

Boggs: You have put your finger on it.

My basketball scam goes down the tubes when two of the players back out. Not only are their feet big, they're cold as hell. I think I had better skedaddle back to Saratoga and keep my nose clean.

For the next weeks I am haunted by the fate of my friend. Friend? Well, hell, all of us because we are so needy and greedy use that word loosely. I am tempted to go back to his apartment and check the place out, see what's happening to all of his stuff, but I am willing to bet my life that the F.B.I. has got a stakeout, and the F.B.I. are the last three people I need to see, although somebody from that agency had already shown up at my apartment to see if I had any information about Marshall's whereabouts, Of course 1 hadn't. I didn't tell them about the letter, either, though it had been post-marked from Arizona.

One morning when I'm experimenting with some special paper for a New Jersey bookie operation—it's the kind of paper that dissolves the moment you toss it into water, the kind of paper used during World War II for secret maps, the kind of thing any bookie would give his eye teeth to get his hands on—and Lorraine wanders in with the morning papers. The headline in the *News* reads:

OSWALD CLONE SLAIN ON DALLAS STREET

Dramatic, but not very accurate. Never in my wildest imagination, which I admit can get pretty wild, did I consider Marshall an Oswald Clone. He was his own man. Weird, but himself. Off the wall, but himself. I don't think Oswald would have taken the trouble to pay back a 5G loan. And now somebody, it was not clear who, had gunned him down.

The rest of the story gave a few details: name, age, a bit of background, how the deceased had in his back pocket a leaflet saying Hands Off Cuba, something from the Fair Play for Cuba Committee. The reporter noted that Marshall died as the result of two perforating gunshot wounds inflicted by high-velocity projectiles, most likely fired from a point behind and somewhat above the level of the deceased. What he was doing in Dallas, I had no idea. The story concluded by noting that the deceased was survived by no known relatives.

Naturally there was no way I was going to show up at the funeral.

"Dr. Perry noted the massive wound of the head."

Two years or so later, I'm back in the bar where the words *Marshall has recovered from his illness* had once been prominent, but now were no longer in sight, and the television is playing one of those game shows where contestants show off all their knowledge of esoteric information, as if all knowledge is not esoteric if you don't know it, when one of the questions is, and get this: "Who invented the can opener?"

My jaw hit the floor.

A tracheotomy was performed. Moe D., who has finally gotten his finances straightened out and has dragged his bloated carcass out of hiding, was standing next to me quaffing his beer. He turns to me and says, "You know, that reminds me."

"Reminds you of what?"

"Of our friend Marshall."

"Yeah?"

"I always thought it weird about that letter he wrote to Ted Kennedy. You know, the letter that was printed in the papers?"

"What about it?"

"It wasn't in Marshall's handwriting."

"What are you talking about?"

"I tell you, the writing in that letter does not match any of the writing I have from Marshall."

"You're crazy!"

"No. I'm not. You want me to prove it to you?"

"Right," I say. "Just what the world needs. Another conspiracy theory. Under every bush a conspiracy."

Moe D., whose head is bald, pushes with both arms away from the bar. It's the only exercise he gets. That plus running away from his creditors. The last exercise alone should keep him in shape for the rest of his life.

"I didn't say it was a conspiracy. Did I say it was a conspiracy?"

"Then if he didn't write the note, who did? And who killed him?"

"He was probably killed because of the can opener."

"What do you mean the can opener? He bought it for five grand, didn't he?"

"No, he didn't buy it for five grand." He puts two fingers up into the air to order another round of whatever we think we're drinking. I don't even care anymore. None of the contestants on the quiz show knows who invented the can opener. I don't either.

"He just took the five grand from you," Moe says, "so he could get out to Texas, live in grand style for a few days, and then steal the damn thing."

"He stole it?"

"What do you think?"

"I thought he bought it with the money I loaned him."

"Naah, he stole it." Moe D. wipes the beer foam from his upper lip.

Mad Dog would be a good nickname for him. "They probably killed him because he stole their goddamn can opener."

"Who's they?"

"I don't know *who's they*." Moe D. shrugs his massive shoulders. "It's the fate of all those Kennedy investigators, isn't it?"

I make a sour face. "Marshall? Marshall wasn't an investigator. He was just a collector."

"So you say. Where's his collection now?"

It's my turn to shrug. "I have no idea."

Moe D. shakes his head. Maybe whatever is inside rattles. "I went back to his apartment not long after the letter was printed in the paper, and Marshall's apartment was completely cleaned out. Everything gone."

"You're crazy."

"Am I?"

We stare into our beers. The game show continues.

"Even the can opener?"

Moe D. nods. We drink. Finally the football game comes on and we get engrossed in more immediate topics.

"The body is that of a muscular, well-developed and well-nourished adult Caucasian male measuring 72 1/2 inches and weighing approximately 170 pounds," says the announcer as the quarterback runs onto the field.

"There is beginning *rigor mortis.* . . ."

Yeah. Yeah. There is *rigor mortis* all over this land of ours. *Livor mortis* of the *dorsum* and early *algor mortis.* All over our land. My country 'tis of thee I sing.

The basic text:

See the President ride in a car.

See the President greet the people.

See the President wave his hat.

See the President get shot

Run, Spot, run.

Run, Oswald, run.

Run, Tippit, run.

Louis Phillips, a widely published poet, playwright, and short story writer has written some 35 books for children and adults. Among his works are two collections of short stories—*A Dream of Countries Where No One Dare Live* (SMU Press) and *The Bus to the Moon* (Fort Schuyler Press); *Hot Corner*, a collection of his baseball writings, and *R. I. P.* (a sequence of poems about Rip Van Winkle) from Livingston Press; *The Envoi Messages*, a full-length play (Broadway Play Publishers) and *The Audience Book of Theatre Quotations* (World Audience, Inc.). His books for children include *The Man Who Stole the Atlantic Ocean* (Prentice Hall & Camelot Books), *The Million Dollar Potato* (Simon and Schuster), and *How to Wrestle an Alligator* (Avon). His sequence of poems—*The Time, The Hour, The Solitariness of the Place*—was the co-winner in the Swallow's Tale Press competition (1984). Among his published books of poems are *The Krazy Kat Rag* (Light Reprint Press), *Bulkington* (Hollow Spring Press), *Celebrations & Bewilderments* (Fragments Press), *In the Field of Broken Hearts*, and *Into the Well of Knowingness* (Prologue Press). He teaches at the School of Visual Arts in NYC.

Acknowledgments

Writing was the winner of the 1994 *Nassau Review* Short Story Award. The following stories in this collection also were published originally in *The Nassau Review*: *Notes From the Committee of Grief*, *The Gorilla and My Wife*, *The Interpretations of Dreams*, *The Cat that Swallowed Thomas Hardy's Heart*, *In America, You Do Not Understand Your Life Unless You Understand the Movies*, and *The Woman Who Wrote King Lear*.

The Destruction of Iowa appeared originally in *The Mississippi Valley Review.*

The Case of John Locke's Bicycle appeared originally in *The Crescent Review.*

Suddenly I Do Not Equate the Light With Anything But Madness: The Best Short Story of 2010 appeared originally in *Thrust: Experimental and Underground Prose.*

The author would also like to express deep appreciation to the following persons who helped make these stories and this collection possible: Paul Doyle, editor of *The Nassau Review*; Robert Karmon; Christopher McMillan; Patrice Boyle who typed a number of the stories; Mac Bica who, with great patience and understanding shares an office with me at The School of Visual Arts.

And, last, but not least, Jack Estes who read and reread every story carefully and still decided to publish this collection.

Books from *Pleasure Boat Studio: A Literary Press*

(*Note*: Caravel Books is a new imprint of Pleasure Boat Studio: A Literary Press. Caravel Books is the imprint for mysteries only. Aequitas Books is another imprint which includes non-fiction with philosophical and sociological themes. Empty Bowl Press is a Division of Pleasure Boat Studio.)

UPCOMING: *The Shadow in the Water* • Inger Frimansson, trans. fm. Swedish by Laura Wideburg • a caravel mystery
UPCOMING: *Immortality* • Mike O'Connor
UPCOMING: *Working the Woods, Working the Sea* • an empty bowl book
UPCOMING: *Listening to the Rhino* • Dr. Janet Dallett • an aequitas book

Weinstock Among the Dying • Michael Blumenthal • fiction • $18
The War Journal of Lila Ann Smith • Irving Warner • historical fiction • $18
Dream of the Dragon Pool: A Daoist Quest • Albert A. Dalia • fantasy • $18
Good Night, My Darling • Inger Frimansson, Trans by Laura Wideburg • $18 • a caravel mystery
Falling Awake: An American Woman Gets a Grip on the Whole Changing World—One Essay at a Time • Mary Lou Sanelli • $15 • non-fiction • an aequitas book
Way Out There: Lyrical Essays • Michael Daley • $16 • non-fiction • an aequitas book
The Case of Emily V. • Keith Oatley • $18 • a caravel mystery
Monique • Luisa Coehlo, Trans fm Portuguese by Maria do Carmo de Vasconcelos and Dolores DeLuise • fiction • $14
The Blossoms Are Ghosts at the Wedding • Tom Jay • essays and poems • $15 • an empty bowl book
Against Romance • Michael Blumenthal • poetry • $14
Speak to the Mountain: The Tommie Waites Story • Dr. Bessie Blake • 278 pages • biography • $18 / $26 • an aequitas book
Artrage • Everett Aison • fiction • $15
Days We Would Rather Know • Michael Blumenthal • poetry • $14
Puget Sound: 15 Stories • C. C. Long • fiction • $14
Homicide My Own • Anne Argula • fiction (mystery) • $16
Craving Water • Mary Lou Sanelli • poetry • $15
When the Tiger Weeps • Mike O'Connor • poetry and prose • 15
Wagner, Descending: The Wrath of the Salmon Queen • Irving Warner • fiction • $16
Concentricity • Sheila E. Murphy • poetry • $13.95
Schilling, from a study in lost time • Terrell Guillory • fiction • $16.95
Rumours: A Memoir of a British POW in WWII • Chas Mayhead • nonfiction • $16
The Immigrant's Table • Mary Lou Sanelli • poetry and recipes • $13.95
The Enduring Vision of Norman Mailer • Dr. Barry H. Leeds • criticism • $18
Women in the Garden • Mary Lou Sanelli • poetry • $13.95
Pronoun Music • Richard Cohen • short stories • $16
If You Were With Me Everything Would Be All Right • Ken Harvey • short stories • $16
The 8th Day of the Week • Al Kessler • fiction • $16
Another Life, and Other Stories • Edwin Weihe short stories • $16
Saying the Necessary • Edward Harkness • poetry • $14
Nature Lovers • Charles Potts • poetry • $10
In Memory of Hawks, & Other Stories from Alaska • Irving Warner • fiction • $15
The Politics of My Heart • William Slaughter • poetry • $12.95

The Rape Poems • Frances Driscoll • poetry • $12.95
When History Enters the House: Essays from Central Europe • Michael Blumenthal • nonfiction • $15
Setting Out: The Education of Lili • Tung Nien • Trans fm Chinese by Mike O'Connor • fiction • $15

Our Chapbook Series:

No. 1: *The Handful of Seeds: Three and a Half Essays* • Andrew Schelling • $7 • nonfiction
No. 2: *Original Sin* • Michael Daley • $8 • poetry
No. 3: *Too Small to Hold You* • Kate Reavey • $8 • poetry
No. 4: *The Light on Our Faces: A Therapy Dialogue* • Lee Miriam WhitmanRaymond • $8 • poetry
No. 5: *Eye* • William Bridges • $8
No. 6: *Selected* New Poems *of Rainer Maria Rilke* • Trans fm German by Alice Derry • $10 • poetry
No. 7: *Through High Still Air: A Season at Sourdough Mountain* • Tim McNulty • $9 • poetry and prose
No. 8: *Sight Progress* • Zhang Er, Trans fm Chinese by Rachel Levitsky • $9 • prosepoems
No. 9: *The Perfect Hour* • Blas Falconer • $9 • poetry
No. 10: Fervor • Zaedryn Meade • $10 • poetry

From other publishers (in limited editions):

Desire • Jody Aliesan • $14 • poetry (an Empty Bowl book)
Deams of the Hand • Susan Goldwitz • $14 • poetry (an Empty Bowl book)
Lineage • Mary Lou Sanelli • $14 • poetry (an Empty Bowl book)
The Basin: Poems from a Chinese Province • Mike O'Connor • $10 / $20 • poetry (paper/ hardbound) (an Empty Bowl book)
The Straits • Michael Daley • $10 • poetry (an Empty Bowl book)
In Our Hearts and Minds: The Northwest and Central America • Ed. Michael Daley • $12 • poetry and prose (an Empty Bowl book)
The Rainshadow • Mike O'Connor • $16 • poetry (an Empty Bowl book)
Untold Stories • William Slaughter • $10 / $20 • poetry (paper / hardbound) (an Empty Bowl book)
In Blue Mountain Dusk • Tim McNulty • $12.95 • poetry (a Broken Moon book)
China Basin • Clemens Starck • $13.95 • poetry (a Story Line Press book)
Journeyman's Wages • Clemens Starck • $10.95 • poetry (a Story Line Press book)

Orders. Pleasure Boat Studio books are available by order from your bookstore, directly from PBS, or through the following:
SPD (Small Press Distribution) Tel. 8008697553, Fax 5105240852
Partners/West Tel. 4252278486, Fax 4252042448
Baker & Taylor Tel. 8007751100, Fax 8007757480
Ingram Tel. 6157935000, Fax 6152875429
Amazon.com or **Barnesandnoble.com**

Pleasure Boat Studio: A Literary Press
201 West 89th Street
New York, NY 10024
Tel / Fax: 8888105308
www.pleasureboatstudio.com / *pleasboat@nyc.rr.com*

Printed in the United States
115557LV00001B/241-276/P